WATER  ILD

Jo Zebedee

Inspired
Quill

Published by Inspired Quill: July 2017

First Edition

Chief Editor: Rebecca Hall
Cover Design: Venetia Jackson
Typeset in Dante

Paperback ISBN: 978-1-908600-61-5
eBook ISBN: 978-1-908600-62-2
Print Edition

Printed in the United Kingdom
1 2 3 4 5 6 7 8 9 10

Inspired Quill Publishing, UK
Business Reg. No. 7592847
www.inspired-quill.com

Praise for Jo Zebedee

"Definitely an author to watch out for."

– Tim C Taylor,
author of the *Human Legion* series

"Writes characters so close you could touch them."

– Dan Jones,
author of *Man O'War*

"A bright and fresh new voice in the genre, brimming with imagination, subtle world building and engaging characters."

– Francis (Julia) King,
author of *Fade to Black*

"From first word to last, a pleasure to read."

– J L Dobias,
author of *The Crippled Mode* series

"A dark fable about belonging that is rooted as deeply in Northern Ireland as it is in the fantasy genre, with shades of Graham Joyce thrown in for good measure."

– Stephen Poore,
Gemmell Award Longlisted

"Waters and the Wild had me in suspense from the first page to the last. Ancient legends meet the modern world in a powerful tale of haunting ambiguities."

– Teresa Edgerton,
author of the *Green Lion* Trilogy

"Waters and the Wild is a sinister, heart-stopping tale of fairy abduction in the beautiful glens of Antrim. You need it. So read it."

– Peadar O'Guilin,
The Call

To Mum, who introduced me to reading,
and to Yeats, amongst many other greats.

PROLOGUE

I NEVER KNEW *panic could make ice jump into my throat and cold fingers crawl up my spine. That it could change me from a rational, normal mum, unpacking in the caravan at the start of our holiday, into a harridan who screamed at my husband for losing our daughter; at my young, stunned son for needing me; at the police to do something – anything – to find her.*

That was the first time, the time when everything changed, and the memory never fades: Phil running through the site, Mark beside him on coltish legs, struggling to keep up. Phil's panicked eyes meeting mine, Phil who'd always been strong. He ran up to where I was, standing on the caravan's step clutching a pair of tiny dungarees, just perfect for a five-year-old girl. Before he spoke I knew he'd been away too long and … I knew.

"Amy's gone," he said, his words strained. He sucked in a breath. "We need to call the police."

"Gone where?" I didn't scream or yell. Not then. It wasn't real yet.

"From the little glen," he said. "The one at the top of the site."

Amy's glen, where she'd spent the last summer enchanted by 'fairies'. We'd encouraged her game, not knowing, then, what it

1

was really about.

Mark had been the one with the sense to run to the rangers' lodge, and the ranger on duty called the police. All Phil could say, over and over, was that it wasn't possible for her to be gone, that he'd been watching her, that there was no way out of the glen. Mark agreed and the bile rose in me because – it was *possible; they had lost her.*

The search went on all night. Helicopters droned over the forest. Floodlights swept the glen. Voices shouted: "Amy! Amy!" An officer gave her description on the radio; they thought someone had taken her. Another asked for a photo, and when I didn't have one they called my parents. I watched lights dance over the forest, back and forth, and couldn't focus on anything except the creeping knowledge that I wouldn't see her again.

They found her after dark, in the glen, curled under an overhang of trees. Someone came to the van where we were having another cup of tea – I've never drunk tea since – and I ran across the site, the grass whipping my ankles. I climbed the stile into the glen beyond. A policewoman helped me over; she was shaking her head, saying it was a miracle, that no one knew how they'd missed her. I heard Phil ask where she'd been found, heard him say he'd bloody known there was no way past. Clever Mark checked it really was Amy.

I left all that behind and walked into the circle of police. There, in the middle of the officers, her face dimpling when she saw me, Amy waited. The ice in me broke – shattered – and I ran to her. I picked her up and spun her round until she laughed.

"Where did you go, sweetie?" I asked when I put her down. I crouched in front of her and gave her a box of raisins – I knew she'd be hungry. As she went to take the raisins I saw something in her hand: a golden acorn, perfect except for a crack in its side, its metal catching the moonlight.

"Where did you get that?"

"From the fairies," she said, her eyes solemn. "I found it."

My heart stilled. Amy never lied. Phil, now beside me, bent in front of her and stroked her hand. I watched, tense, as he said, "Tell the truth, honey."

"I did." She gave a little smile, a dancing one, and said, "I was with the fairies."

Mark stared at his sister. I saw him taking in her eyes, her hair, the cunning smile. He looked her up and down and then grinned, an eight-year-old's grin that wasn't scared like mine.

"Cool," he said, drawing out the word. "Can I be their prince?"

But he wasn't their prince: he couldn't be anything to them. They only ever wanted Amy.

CHAPTER ONE

THE BRIDGE TO the waterfall was deserted: the last of the tourists were either eating dinner in the nearby restaurant, or away back to their cars. Thank God; if Simon heard once more how cute the glen was or how quaint the Irish, he might throw himself in the river and have done with it. He looped his hands over the railing, his eyes half closing.

The waterfall that attracted the tourists to Glenariff drummed, far in the distance. He was half tempted to wander up one of the two paths leading to it, but even on a good day the wooden walkways were shaded and mossy. After the afternoon's rain and in the falling darkness, they'd be lethal. A dove cooed and settled to roost in the trees, the forest's stillness making its call seem louder than it ought to be. Simon swayed a little and grabbed the railing: he'd definitely had too much to drink.

The sound of footsteps jerked him awake. He turned to see a girl of about eighteen walking past the restaurant's glass windows. Her dress, a gossamer, floral job, stuck to her legs and her dark jacket merged with the surrounding trees, making her look like she'd stepped out of the forest instead of the reception.

She stopped at the end of the bridge and cocked her head. A moment later, she nodded and started to cross, the sharp heels of her sandals making a pit-pit sound on the wood. As she passed Simon, her hands fluttered at her side. She took no notice of him, intent on an internal conversation. He smothered a smile. The fizzy wine had been flowing just as liberally as the Guinness all day. In fact, one bright spark had combined both to make Black Velvet cocktails, and handed them out as a dare.

The girl half-stumbled onto the well-worn path beyond the bridge. Trees crowded it, making it dark enough for a line of floodlights to illuminate, highlighting the pretty ferns but nothing practical like the path. Speaking of practical – the girl teetered in her strappy sandals.

"Hey!" Simon skidded as he crossed the still-wet bridge. "Wait up!"

She turned. Her eyes widened. "I didn't see you."

"No. You were—" Distracted or pissed, which would offend less? He shrugged; best not to go there. "Where are you going?"

"To the waterfall." She backed away: coltish, tense.

He stopped a few feet from her. Was he scaring her? He didn't see how he could be. "You can't go up there." He kept his voice soft. "Even the yanks aren't daft enough to go up at night."

She didn't smile at his poor joke. "I've got good night vision."

She'd need to be an owl. Disco lights came on in the function room behind him, reflecting in her eyes, making them sharper, more aware. He wasn't sure she *was* drunk. Either way, there was no way he could let her go up on her own. If she didn't fall, she'd catch her death of cold, especially if the rain came back on. He opened his hands in a non-threatening way. "Look, Miss… what's your name?"

"Amy." She raised her chin, meeting his eyes, almost defiant. "Amy Lyle."

Ah, now he knew why he'd recognised her. It may have been fifteen years since he'd last seen her but she was hard to forget. Or, at least, the look on his ma's face was.

"I'm Simon McCormick. You hid under your ma's skirt at my uncle's funeral and showed her knickers to the entire church when you came out. My ma still dines out on the story."

Actually, Ma had talked about the Lyles recently, but he couldn't bring the details to mind. A divorce? Something like that.

"I don't remember you," she said. "All I remember is the skirt incident – Mum never lets me forget." She smiled, obviously not sorry. "So, we're related or something?"

"Something," he said. "Cousins fifteen times removed at best." He nodded up the path. "Do you have to go to the waterfall tonight? It's getting dark."

Her smile fell away, leaving a pinched, set expression. "Yes." She pulled her jacket tight, hands clenched so her knuckles were white. She turned and set off up the path, quicker than before.

"Jesus, be careful." He made to go after her, but stopped. How would it look to someone back at the wedding party, him chasing a slip of a thing up the glen?

The sound of skidding followed by a soft curse reached his ears.

"Fuck it," he said, and headed up the path after Amy. He caught up with her at the bottom of the wooden walkway leading to the waterfall. The noise of the water had changed, growing deeper and louder as it channeled through a ravine on his left instead of burbling over stones. A rail protected climbers from the ravine, and the cliff-face hugged the other side, casting the walkway into a darkness barely broken by the few lights.

Amy had already started to climb a short flight of steps to the first section.

"Amy, stop," he said. "Look how dark it is."

She paused, her hand on the rail. He counted another two sets of steps before the path twisted out of sight.

"What's so important it can't wait until tomorrow?" he pleaded.

"It's…." Her gaze cast over the ravine, skipping from rock to tree, to the river, to the cliff. "I have to go up." He could only just hear her over the water, her voice was so low. "That's all." She looked tense, almost hungry, in her eager stance, as if listening for something in the forest.

The drumming of the waterfall echoed through the glen. The air was dank, and the woods close and still. The moment stretched. She shouldn't be here, not with the forest watching. He couldn't have said why, just that it didn't feel safe. He wanted to get back to the noise and the reception crowd, away from this empty place.

"If you go, I'll have to follow you," he said. "I wouldn't let anyone walk around here in the dark. But it's been a long day, and I don't fancy the trek." Not to mention that going any further into the wooded glen had started to scare the shit out of him. "I mean, I'm all for stretching my legs after the speeches, but not rock climbing." He was babbling, but at least while she was listening she wasn't leaving. "How can anyone talk for that long? Forty-six minutes? I had a bet on eighteen. I'm down a fiver."

"I chose fourteen," she said, surprising him with a short laugh. "All that guff about soul mates and past lives and carrying love on forever…. And they call *me* nuts."

Did they? Something caught at the edge of his thoughts, buried under all the family info his mother had dumped on him.

Amy glanced up the path. "Is it really too dark to see anything? I thought there might be lights at the fall."

For all he knew the place could be lit up like a beacon. "Yeah. Definitely. Pitch black at the top." He held a hand out. "Shall we go?"

Carefully, he closed the gap between them until she was only inches away. Her perfume reached him, a musk that matched the glen's loamy scent. Combined with her cropped hair and big eyes, she had a sense of other-worldliness that made his breath catch, something almost fairy-like. He cupped her elbow with his hand.

The wind shifted. The trees whispered, urging him to take her into the watching forest. He tightened his grip on her arm. If he helped her up to the waterfall, he could make sure she didn't fall.

He jumped at a sudden blast of music from the reception. What had he been thinking? He let go of her.

The trees were still. The wind's noise died away. Unease settled in his bones; a low warning. "I think we should get out of here."

"Yes." Her eyes were wide, her gaze roving everywhere.

"Come on." He started to guide her down the path,

frightened to rush in case she broke away; scared not to, in case this respite didn't last.

As they reached the bridge, she stopped and looked back the way they'd come. "You were telling the truth about the dark? You're not just humouring me."

"Of course not," he lied. He set off over the bridge, shepherding her along its narrow length. He led her around the corner to the car park and crunched over the gravel to the restaurant. As he opened the door, music pumped into the night and heat from the bar hit his face. He pushed through, claustrophobic under the lounge's low ceiling hung with the paraphernalia the restaurant was famous for: farm equipment, musical instruments, signage of all sorts. Amy flitted past, light on her feet, and went into the function room at the back. There, huge windows looked out to the forest, reflecting the disco lights.

A small dance floor had been cleared but most of the guests were gathered by the bar or sitting at the hastily rearranged tables. He couldn't have been away more than twenty minutes, but it felt like he'd been in the forest for hours.

A woman crossed the dance floor to Amy, lines etched either side of her mouth. "Where were you?" Her shrill voice was loud enough to carry over the music. "I was about to send out a search party." A bloke standing at her shoulder proved her words weren't a joke. He had the same dark eyes as Amy: a brother, Simon decided, and somehow familiar to him. Work, perhaps, or the rugby club.

Amy hunched into her jacket. "I just went to get some air, Mum." Her eyes met Simon's: *don't tell.*

"Did something happen?" Amy's mother's voice was demanding, almost hungry. "Did you see *them*?"

A muscle in Amy's cheek twitched. "Maybe." A look

passed between her and her mother, some kind of common understanding. "But they've gone now."

"Leave it." The brother made an abrupt cutting off motion with his hands. He nodded at the door. "Ralph's trying to get your attention."

"He's giving me a lift back to Belfast," said her mother. "He must want to go."

"I could come too," said Amy. Her eyes drifted to the window. "It might be for the best."

"The car's full," said her mother, her words quick. "Mark will get you home on the bus." She reached for Amy, but her hand caught in the little necklace around her neck, breaking the chain. The pendant slid down the chain, off the end, and spilled onto the dance floor. It would have rolled further but her brother stopped it with his foot.

"Mum!" Amy grabbed the acorn and held it clasped against her. "Be careful."

"No harm done," said the brother, his face strained. "Mum, you had better go before Ralph has an apoplexy." He flashed a quick grin at Amy. "Don't worry. I'll stick close. You won't be able to gallivant off."

Her mother reached out and stroked Amy's cheek. "You can tell me tomorrow all about the night you have." She made her way through the wedding crowd to the door, pushed it open, and left with Ralph and two women. Simon stared after her. Surely the car could take one more?

"Jesus," said Mark, taking his attention. "She's in some form. Except with you, Amy, oh Golden Child." He smiled, and it took the edge off his barbed words.

Amy took a seat at a table close to the window and stared into the blackness beyond, her hand clenched around her pendant. She looked older, sitting there – older and fragile, as if she could break.

Chapter Two

A T MIDNIGHT THE band wrapped up, ignoring a last request for something by the Killers from the drunk, raucous table of women at the front. Or the suggestion the lead singer should take his kit off.

Simon found himself glancing – again – at the table Amy had shared with her brother. Mark hadn't lied about sticking like glue; even when he'd gone to the bar and got chatting, his attention kept going back to her.

Now, both she and her brother were gone. Her jacket and bag – a huge thing patterned with daisies – were hanging on the back of her seat. Presumably the Lyles had joined the toilet queue from hell ahead of the bus to Belfast.

Speaking of which…. Simon shrugged on his suit jacket and removed his buttonhole, leaving the half-wilted carnation on the table beside an empty glass, and joined the queue for the men's. The chat had grown subdued, just the odd comment about the time of night and what a grand day it had been. Somewhere near the front Max, the best man, was loudly slurring his words; now the bride had left he was reverting to his rugby-club form.

Amy's brother emerged from the toilets and looked over at their table. He paled and started to search the room with worried eyes. A moment later, he pushed his way to the queue for the ladies' and spoke to one of the women at the front. She nodded, went into the toilets, and came out a few moments later. At the shake of her head, Mark's lips moved in an unmistakeable curse.

Simon looked out of the picture windows. He remembered Amy's dark eyes looking up the path, fixed on whatever lay at the top, the deep silence as the forest had waited for them. *Oh, crap.* He left the queue and caught up with Mark.

"Has she gone?" he asked.

"Yes." Mark ran his hands through his hair, looking around the room, taking in each table. He set off for the door. "I have to find her."

"I'll help."

"Simon, isn't it? You do web designs?" Finally, Simon placed the other man – he worked in one of the companies he'd designed for. "Check the bar as you go through. But quickly."

Simon followed through to the main bar, and they split up. He weaved in and out between the tables as fast as he could, but there was no Amy. He reached the front door where Mark soon joined him.

"Bollocks," said Mark. "She *has* fucking gone. Jesus Christ, I only left her alone for a minute."

"The waterfall," said Simon. He cleared his throat. "I was chatting to her earlier, and she wanted see it."

"Oh, for Christ's sake." Mark pushed the door open and stepped into the expanse of gravelled car park. He half-ran around the side of the building, stopping on the bridge. His eyes scanned between the two paths leading up to the waterfall. "Amy! Come on, it's Mark! You're not in trouble, I just want to know you're okay."

Nothing came back but the whistle of the wind through the trees.

"Should I get help?" asked Simon.

"No point. You could send a squad after her, and they wouldn't find her unless she wanted them to. She could be beside us and we wouldn't know."

Mark fished a torch out of his suit pocket, and Simon frowned; who in God's name brought a torch to a wedding? Mark must have noticed his surprise, because he gave a quick shrug. "Best to be prepared when you're with our Amy."

The path along the river stretched in front of Simon. He glanced longingly back at the bar.

"You take the left path, I'll take the right." Mark paused. "You got a phone?" Simon nodded. "Right, put in my number. If we get lost we can call." He called out the number, waited while Simon connected with his phone and saved it, and then he was away down the path, shouting his sister's name, cajoling her to come out.

Simon started up the other path. He left the floodlit exterior of the restaurant behind and passed into the full darkness of the glen, only the irregular spotlights lighting his way. The waterfall's noise became a low rumble which settled in the pit of his stomach. From the other side of the ravine Mark continued to call, his voice increasingly urgent. Simon frowned; Amy had only been missing a short time and the two paths followed a loop around the glen. At some point, they had to meet up with her. There was no need to panic.

He kept climbing, alert for any movement. His eyes adjusted to the dark, picking out ghost-grey ferns and the white-foamed water. He clambered up the path. It was less slippery than the other, thankfully, but his feet still went from under him a couple of times, and he kept tight hold of the railing. Finally, he reached the viewing platform. The waterfall crashed on the rocks ahead, floodlit from behind, so the peaty water held a golden sheen.

Mark arrived from the other path and flashed his torch around, picking out rocks and the fine spray hitting Simon's face. The light jerked as Mark pointed it down the river, making no more impact on the dark than the floodlights.

"She's not here," said Simon. "We should go back and get people out to look. Or check the bar again."

No answer, just the incessant sweep of the torchlight. His hair was already soaked through by the spray. He put his hands in his pockets and fought not to shiver. "Come on, mate, she's not here."

Mark turned to him, his dark eyes glinting. "Quiet a minute. I need to listen."

Simon raised an eyebrow but fell quiet in the face of the other man's distress. Now he was used to the noise, the waterfall dominated a little less. He became aware of another sound under the thundering: a sing-song noise, almost a hum.

"She's here," said Mark. "I can hear her."

Simon leaned over the wooden railing, searching the length of the ravine and along the line of both paths. If she was close enough to hear, he should be able to see her. "Where the hell is she?"

Mark shrugged. "She bolts," he said. "She's here, but

she's hidden." He nodded down the path. "Look, why don't you head back? You'll miss the bus, otherwise; there's no one sober enough to stop and do a head-count down there."

Simon paused, tempted. He had no business standing here looking for a girl he'd spoken to for barely ten minutes. He shook his head. It would be pretty low to leave Mark standing out here on his own. Besides – she should have been easy to find. The memory of the glen earlier, how it had infected him, nagged. He couldn't walk away.

"Fuck it. If I miss the bus, it'll save me an hour of interrogation from Aunt Agnes." He leaned against the railings. "I'll wait with you."

"Up to you." The terse words held an edge of relief. Mark cast his torch around once again. The humming grew louder, until Simon could almost place it, but faded just as quickly. The only movement, aside from the water, came from moths fluttering around the floodlights. A chill settled into his bones.

"This is crazy," he said. "She's not here. Look—" He leaned over the wooden rail, trying not to think how deep the gorge it protected him from was. "Amy!" His voice hit the rock and echoed back.

Mark swung his torch, tracking the river. Its light caught something glinting between two of the walkway's planks. Simon leaned forward to pick it up.

"Mark," he said, and held out the little acorn from Amy's necklace.

"Oh, hell." Mark leaned right over the rail. The torchlight bobbed as he searched the gorge, up the rock walls and along the paths. Finally, his voice heavy with relief, he said, "She's there."

He'd caught Amy in the torchlight, on the turn of the

path below. She huddled against the cliff face, shivering in her gossamer dress. Her face was streaked and dirty and her arms scratched so badly long rivulets of blood ran down them, despite the rain.

"Mark." Her voice wavered. "It's happening again."

Chapter Three

"**S**TAY THERE, AMY." Mark hurried to the top of the steps. "I'm on my way."

Simon caught up with him and grabbed his arm. "Where'd she come from?" He gestured around the empty platform. Either they'd missed Amy on the path or she'd followed them up from the restaurant. But she'd been near them, singing, for ages.

"It doesn't matter." Mark skidded down the path, pulling off his suit jacket as he went. When he reached his sister he draped it around her shoulders and tipped her face towards one of the floodlights. "Let's see you."

"I'm all right."

"God, Amy," Mark said. He lifted one of her arms, exposing a long gash. It was nasty, deep and ragged, but she didn't flinch. She had guts, at least. "What happened?"

"They're just scratches. From the brambles."

Simon leaned as far over the railing as he dared. The river was a long way down. She couldn't have climbed up in the dark. He glanced down the path, keen to get out of this place with its questions and lack of answers. If they hurried, the bus might still be there. "We should head down," he said.

"Good idea." Mark straightened. "We need to get you warmed up, Amy."

"Who's that?" Amy peered past her brother, her big eyes reflected in one of the spotlights. She disentangled herself from Mark, her skirt shifting so Simon could see that her legs were gashed, too. She faced Simon. "You were wrong – there were lights at the waterfall."

He tried not to wince, caught in the lie. "Sorry. It's been years since I was here." And he'd had the sense not to visit at night. Her eyes fixed him with a dark gaze, and he found himself looking down, embarrassed. "I didn't want you to get hurt."

"Save the postmortem for later." Mark put his arm around his sister's shoulders and started to help her down the steps. Simon followed, taking care to plant each foot, using the cliff-face as well as the railing for balance. The steps built into the steepest sections weren't too bad but the flatter sections of path between were a lethal mix of mud on rock.

The Lyles, faring better with the torch, moved ahead. It grew darker as the floodlit waterfall disappeared after a steep, twisted section of the walkway. The river roared alongside him.

His hand touched something cold and he jerked away, nearly losing his balance. A rivulet ran down the cliff-face into a dark, still puddle, a couple of inches deep; a fairy's bath, his ma would say. A lot of rubbish, he'd tell her, and ignore her warnings not to laugh at things he didn't understand. Somehow, in the dark glen, where the slightest splash of water had made him jump, her notions didn't seem so funny.

He hurried to the last section of walkway, the steepest yet, slipping and sliding. His shoulders lowered in relief as the wider path leading to the bridge came into view.

Something caught his ankle. He stifled a yell, and looked down to see a bramble lying across the step. He gave a sharp laugh. Jesus, he was jumpy as hell.

He put his foot down, and something sharp, perhaps the end of a branch, caught his hair. It yanked him back and this time he did fall. He hit the edge of the step, hard. He kicked his legs, trying to get a purchase on the slippery ground, but it made no difference. His jacket and shirt rode up his back. Rough wood tore at his skin. His head thudded off one of the steps, jarring his teeth; his back hit the hard edge of another.

"Simon!" shouted Mark. "You all right?"

He landed at the bottom of the steps and dug his heels in, trying to slow down, but his ankle caught against a protruding railing support. It twisted, sending a sharp wrench of pain up his leg.

"Bollocks!" he yelled. He came to a stop and lay, too stunned to move.

Mark appeared a few feet away, his pale shirt ghost-like in the dark. Amy darted past and reached Simon first. She put an arm under his shoulder and helped him sit up. "What happened?"

"Not sure." He leaned forward and rubbed his ankle, trying to hide how much he was shaking. "I slipped." He felt like a dick; he'd had worse during a Saturday morning ruck. Except in a ruck he'd have a physio with magic-spray. "I busted that ankle a couple of months ago. This won't help me get back on the field."

Mark hunkered in front of him. "Can you walk?"

"I think so." Simon moved his leg and pain crazed its way through his muscle. "I might need a hand," he admitted.

"Right." Mark gave Amy the torch and put one arm under Simon's shoulders. "Come on, big lad. Amy, stay with us, okay? I need light, so try to shine it on the path in front."

"Okay." Her gaze skittered around, not settling anywhere for longer than a few seconds.

Mark ducked and got Simon to his feet. He managed to put some of his weight on the ankle. The tendon wasn't torn again, then.

"Hurry." Amy had to walk behind them because of the narrow path, but cast the torch's light a few feet ahead. "We need to hurry."

"All right, calm down." But Mark's voice was thin and nervous. "You're with me now."

They made their way along the final path. Simon put his bad foot down, half-hopping as best he could. They had to get back to the restaurant with its lights and music: back to anywhere that wasn't this knowing glen, with its old trees and quick, golden water.

They reached the bridge, but the restaurant was already closed and dark. Amy pit-patted behind them, a mirror of the earlier evening. They made their way around the corner to the empty car park and stopped at a wooden bench set under some trees. Simon sank onto it. His ankle hurt like a bastard.

He took in the empty car park and closed restaurant and gave a half-laugh, bitten off in disgust.

"Fuck," he said. "They *did* go." He put his head back. "What a bloody night."

Chapter Four

"WHAT NOW?" ASKED Simon. He shivered, either from the cold air or shock from his fall, and put his hands in his pockets, not wanting the Lyles to see how unsettled he'd become.

"We'll have to get a taxi. Christ knows what that'll cost at this time of the night." Mark pulled a phone from his pocket. "Reception isn't great."

"The glen probably blocks the signal," said Simon. Amy shivered beside him, her arms crossed over her stomach for warmth. His ankle ached, and something warm and sticky trickled down his back. He'd be lucky if a taxi would allow him in, and he'd definitely get landed with a cleaning bill. "Anyhow, we don't need a taxi. We need to get sorted out."

Mark sucked at his bottom lip. The wind got up, sending leaves tumbling across the car park, and he gave a sharp nod. This wasn't the place to wait an hour for a Belfast taxi to reach them, and Simon couldn't see the local firm accepting a sixty mile trip on a Saturday night.

"The staff can't all be gone," said Mark. "I'll see if they

can suggest somewhere to stay." He paused, shifting his weight from foot to foot. "Look…. It's important they don't know Amy went up the glen."

"Why?"

"My mother's odd about things like that. I don't want word getting back to her." He looked as if he was going to say something else, but snapped his mouth closed instead.

"She's odd about what, exactly?" asked Simon. Mountain climbing at midnight, or something more general? It was time for some answers. He turned to Amy. "Why did you go back to the waterfall?"

"I was called," she said. Her chin came up, defiant.

Christ, it just kept getting better. "By what?"

"The fairies." She was completely serious. "I know it sounds nuts, but I hear them. I always have."

"Fairies. Right." Simon imagined his mother and how she'd react if *he* decided to go after fairies. She wouldn't want anyone to know, either. "I can see what your ma means. I won't say what happened."

"Cheers." Mark pocketed his phone and tucked his hands under his armpits. "Amy, sit there while I get help. Don't go anywhere. *Please.*"

"Okay." Her voice was small and tired.

"Shouldn't you take her with you?" asked Simon. Quite aside from the crazy fairy thing, if she took off again there was no way he'd catch her with his ankle banged up.

"No. If the staff see her scratches, they'll know something happened."

"What if they ask why we're still here?"

Mark shrugged. "I'll tell them that you wandered off pissed and we missed the bus looking for you."

Simon spluttered. "Me?"

"Yeah, you." He walked off, his gait jaunty.

Amy pulled her brother's jacket around her with shaking hands, covering the worst of the scrapes on her arms. Simon found himself softening a little. She'd had a hell of a night, too.

"You all right?" he asked.

She nodded, but didn't meet his eyes. He should tell her she'd been stupid and put them all at risk, but there was no point; she obviously knew. The silence stretched. She fidgeted. Her eyes flitted to the path leading to the glen. Any minute now, she'd be up and away again: he'd put money on it. Rare anger built; *someone* needed to make her see sense, and her brother hadn't even tried.

"Look at us." He fought to keep his voice steady. "You're ripped to bits, and I've busted my ankle."

"Did you really slip?" Her eyes penetrated the darkness, sharp, missing nothing. At least her focus had come away from the glen. "Don't lie. I hate it when people lie to me."

He thought about how the bramble had been like icy fingers on his ankle, and paused, on the verge of telling her. He shook his head; her notions were bad enough, without him adding to them. "Of course I slipped."

She held his gaze for a moment and he managed not to look away. She hunched forward, shivering so much the bench rattled.

"You can lean against me," he said, carefully; she was tense as a cat. "I don't bite. I assume you don't either."

"I never have so far." She settled against his shoulder and he put his arm around her. Her shivers eased. The river gurgled behind them. In the distance an owl hooted, making the the night feel oddly peaceful. Amy obviously wasn't your conventional mad woman. In fact, when she wasn't off on fairy hunts she seemed normal enough.

He became aware of her breathing, the soft rise and fall of her shoulders. Her leg was against his, stealing his warmth. He tightened his hold on her and she leaned against him, seemingly asleep. It moved him, somehow – to be trusted like this, to be the person someone would nestle against. His eyes sagged.

The sound of footsteps crunching over gravel woke him. Amy was asleep, snuggled against his shirt, marking it with either dirt or makeup, so it looked even more like a dishrag rather than something that had cost a fortune for the wedding.

"Can you walk?" asked Mark.

Amy stirred and sat up. Simon swallowed a tinge of disappointment. "How far?"

Mark pointed at a line of three cars at the opposite side of the car park. "The manager's sister runs a holiday house up the coast a bit. She'll put us up. He's going to give us a lift."

"Yeah, I can manage that." Simon got to his feet, and his ankle protested with a single shot of pain. Whatever he'd done wasn't too bad. He thought of his head hitting the step, the struggle to stop himself. He'd got off lightly. "No probs."

"Good." Mark peered at Amy. "Keep my jacket pulled around you so he won't see the cuts and stay curled against me." He handed her jacket and bag over. "You left those in the bar. Use the bag as a pillow and hide your face, like you're pissed."

"We could just tell them she slipped," said Simon. Mark's possessive attitude towards his sister irked Simon, no matter how much he told himself it was nothing to do with him.

"I'll be telling them nothing. It's no one's business."

A man stepped out of the restaurant and jingled his keys. "Come on, then." He looked resigned to the night's events, and waited patiently for Simon to walk – well, mostly hop, but movement was movement – to the car.

"Are you the one who went up the glen?" The man laughed. "What were you after, leprechauns?"

Simon shot Mark a dirty look and opened the passenger door. An assortment of crisp wrappers, plastic bags and empty coke cans littered the well of the seat.

"Sorry – kids." The driver slid behind the wheel. "I had a couple of tourists from Sweden in the bar the other day." He reversed in a tight circle that sent loose stones pinging against the car. "They were convinced they saw elves up at the waterfall. I told them you had to be a buck eejit to think that." He paused and Simon tensed, waiting for the punchline. "But even they weren't stupid enough to go up at night to see…"

Fucking hilarious. Simon put his head back and zoned out. How the hell had he got himself into this? His ma would say it was because he was too nice, as usual – a soft touch. For once, she might have a point.

CHAPTER FIVE

T HEY TOOK THE inland road, the engine protesting as
they climbed the glen. The sea came into sight, white
horses in the darkness, threatening a storm. The car purred
along, headlights cutting the laneways, until they crossed a
short bridge and stopped outside a whitewashed cottage.

Simon opened the door and stepped out, ignoring a
dog's distant barks. His feet slipped in the mud. He wrinkled
his nose: the cottage was part of a farm set-up, it seemed –
he could make out the shape of a bigger farmhouse just
beyond the cottage. There were no streetlights. Instead,
stars pricked the sky, ending abruptly in a dark line,
presumably the ridge of the glen. Night was never like this
in Belfast, with its streetlights to soften the starkness.

The door to the cottage opened, spilling brightness over
the yard. A woman in a fluffy dressing gown leaned against
the doorjamb.

"May, thanks for doing this," said the driver. "This buck
eejit with the limp decided to go leprechaun hunting in the
glen."

Jesus, this had gone far enough. "I didn't –" Simon glanced to the side. Amy had her head buried against Mark's chest. Mark met Simon's eyes, almost pleading. Fuck it, it was only for one night, and he'd never see the landlady or the driver again. He sighed and gave his best smile, the sort he used on his various aunts, and limped forwards. "I didn't know how far up the glen I'd gone."

"Ach, you're not the first waif I've had turn up." The woman looked tired but her smile seemed genuine. "Come in, and I'll get you beds for the night." She looked Simon up and down. "It'll have been the booze that led you astray. Devil's poison it is."

"Um." Heat rose in his cheeks, but he didn't bother to argue; he must smell like a brewery. The three of them followed her along a narrow corridor, laid with a floral carpet, to one of two open doors.

"That's the double. The other is a twin, so two of you'se will have to share."

Mark nodded. "I'll share with my sister."

Simon frowned: surely it would be more logical for her to have her own room. He took in how close Mark stood against her, his watchful eyes: fuck it, if he wanted to be that protective, it was up to him.

The woman looked closer at Amy. "Is she all right?"

Amy made a small noise and buried her face into Mark's shirt.

"Aye. She drank a bit too much as well. It was a wild day altogether." Mark pulled his phone from his pocket and frowned. "Can I get any coverage here? My ma will be worried about us."

"Ach, no. The ridge cuts off the reception, but there's a payphone in the downstairs hall you can use." She stepped back. "If you need anything else, let me know."

The woman thudded down the stairs, Mark in tow. Amy entered the double room and sat on the edge of the bed. Her face was pale and drawn, her hair lank. Nothing at all like the faerie-girl who'd turned up on the bridge earlier. She must be shattered.

Mark's voice drifted up the stairs: everything was fine, they'd missed the bus that was all. Well, yes, a wee turn, but she was grand now, and they'd be home tomorrow. No, not to worry, Amy was with him. His clipped voice went through the motions, nothing more.

"You shouldn't listen in," said Amy.

Simon closed the door. *A wee turn*? He tried to imagine what a big turn might look like on her, and decided he never wanted to know.

"No, I suppose I shouldn't," he said. "How're your arms – the scratches? And your legs?"

She took off Mark's coat and Simon hissed at the ragged cuts running the length of her arms. Her feet were torn and bloodied, too, and the strap of one of her sandals had worked loose so it dangled from her ankle.

"Shit." He looked around the room – plain, thank God, he hated flowery guff – and saw a white gloss-painted door in the corner. He limped over, and it opened onto a bathroom with a small sink, toilet, and surprisingly swish shower. He lifted one of two flannels, wet and soaped it.

"This'll sting," he warned as he went back to Amy.

She nodded. "It's all right. I'm tough, me."

He paused, taking in the gashes; she was, at that. He managed to get onto his knees and lifted her right foot, the one with the loose sandal. He pulled the sandal off, aware of a door opening and closing down the corridor. Gently, he washed her foot, taking care not to hurt her, running the flannel over her instep and along the side. As he cleaned he saw the scratches weren't too bad; the streaks were mostly mud. He finished and lifted her other foot, doing the same.

When he looked up she was watching him, her eyes shadowed and dark. He swallowed and looked away, confused. She'd caused him so much trouble tonight he should be angry, but when she looked at him, he felt like none of it mattered. He found himself massaging the side of her foot, his thumb moving in small circles. The night hung around them, late and deep.

"Are you coming, Amy?" Mark's voice cut through the silence. He was propped in the now-open doorway, his eyes on Simon. There was no way to tell how long he'd been watching.

Simon let go of Amy's foot. He hadn't been doing anything wrong. He shouldn't feel guilty. But he didn't say anything in his defence – no words seemed to fit that long moment.

"Come on," said Mark. "I don't know about anyone else, but I'm knackered."

Simon handed Amy her sandals and she followed Mark from the room. He pulled himself to his feet and sank onto the edge of the bed. He prised off his right shoe and prodded his ankle, wincing at a sudden burst of pain. It probably needed strapping but he didn't fancy getting May out of her bed again, especially when a night's sleep would keep the weight off it anyway.

He limped to the bathroom and unbuttoned his shirt, peeling it from his skin. Turning, he caught sight of his back in the mirror, scratched to the top of his trousers, angry red lines that resembled Amy's so closely they could be twinned.

He shrugged off the rest of his clothes and groaned as he turned the showerhead so the hot water hit his lower back. Remembering the hard ground that had torn his skin as he had slid, he forced himself to take the flannel and rub the cuts. If Amy could manage without complaining, so could he. Pink water splashed around his feet. He scrubbed again, and once more, until the water ran clean. That would have to do; he was dead on his feet. He wrapped a towel round his waist and pushed his hair back so hard that the water slashed the wall behind.

He hopped into bed and turned off the light. The guesthouse was still, just the rhythmic creak of the guttering reminding him he was somewhere unfamiliar. His thoughts wandered, revisiting the night, sleep-confused images of the wedding, the speeches, the glen.

Was Amy in bed, or was she watching over Glenariff, listening for the voices that had called her? There was no way to escape sight of the glen – it stretched for miles. His eyes snapped open, not sure where that thought had come from. She'd been so small in the darkness, shadowed by the trees, her voice drowned out by the thundering water. Earlier, in the evening's gloom, they'd both understood something out there was watching them, something carried on the breeze that rifled through the trees. How had he felt so in tune with her?

He hoped she managed to sleep; if she did, she might feel better in the morning and whatever she had heard would be gone. He closed his eyes, waiting for sleep to tug him under.

The image of Amy huddling in the dark flashed up, replaced after a moment by the memory of slipping. It *had* felt like something had pulled him down.

He sat up, shivering. *Jesus, get a grip*. He'd caught himself on a bramble, that was all. Even so, he reached across to the bedside table and turned the lamp back on. He lay, checking under his slitted lids from time to time. Nothing moved in the white-painted room; no sound came except the creak-creak of the gutters and the drumming rain – the promised storm had arrived.

It was ridiculous to be so spooked. Grown men didn't sleep with the light on. He reached for the off-switch, but stopped, remembering the darkness surrounding the house, deep and absolute, how the ridge behind had cut off the starlight. Tonight, he did.

CHAPTER SIX

A MY PULLED THE duvet up to her chin and lay facing the ceiling, her acorn clasped in her right hand. Let it keep her safe and hold the voices at bay. She couldn't believe *it* was happening again. She'd taken every pill given, and had seen therapists until her mother's insistence they weren't helping had grown too determined to ignore. She meditated, used mindfulness and thought disruption; everything to hold the voices at bay. After three years of resisting, to the point where they were a nuisance more than disruptive, she thought she had beaten them.

Already asleep in the other bed, Mark's soft breaths blew steady and quiet. It reminded her of when the two had shared a cabin on their dad's boat. They hadn't done that for years, not since Mark had hit his teens and decided sleeping anywhere near his kid sister was mortifying. Except once, after the voices in Strangford Lough. Fear seized her. She tried not to think of that time and neither Mark nor her dad ever referred to it. Tonight, she guessed Mark didn't want her out of his sight. She wasn't the only one with memories.

She thought of Simon, lying in the room next door. If she'd been on her own, she'd have jumped at every bump outside, sure that it – the voices, the crawling knowledge of eyes on her – was going to happen again. Here, she could tell herself the gentle whispering was nothing other than the wind in the eaves and, should it become anything more solid, she'd wake Mark.

She ached from climbing up the ravine, something she wouldn't want to repeat in a hurry. One of her fingernails throbbed from having been pulled right back. She tried to focus on that, and not let her mind wander.

The fairies had grown stronger. Tonight they'd been more than the whispers she was used to. She'd seen them. One had taken her hand and led her to the middle of the stream – not a ravine, in their world, but a babbling river of golden water – and made her dance. Hadn't they? The circling fear that her mother was right, not the doctors, grew in the darkness.

Slowly, her eyes closed and sleep started to take her. The image of the little glen at the caravan site of her childhood, sun dappling the patch of clovered grass she'd liked to play tea parties on, came to her as she slipped under.

Suddenly she was five again, going into the little glen with Dad and Mark. Something glittered at the corner of her eye, a beat-beat of wings that might have been butterflies or, when the light fell towards night-time, powdery moths. The summer before, when she'd first found the glen, fairies had visited her tea parties. She'd been afraid they hadn't been real, and that they would never come back to her. The year waiting to return had been an agony of wishes – on her birthday, at the wishing well in Santa's Grotto, catching dandelion clocks in the wind, each wish had been to see the fairies again.

Mark unpacked his new fishing set, telling Dad what he planned to catch. No one was paying any attention to her. Excitement bubbled in her stomach, a fluttering not unlike the fairies' wings. She strained her ears, sure she'd hear the singing that had been the music to her tea-parties the year before. But she heard nothing except the soft splash of Mark's line, a rustle as her dad settled down with a book and stretched out in a patch of sunlight.

Tears choked her. She'd been sure the fairies would come and ask her to dance. She'd worn her special flared dress so they could see how practiced she'd become; how when she twirled, a final, almost hidden, twist of her waist kept it going.

She left, following the grassy path alongside the stream. She was careful to keep away from Mark, lifting his line from the water and dropping it back in so quickly fish would never go near it. The route led to a shallow pond and she sat beside it, balancing on a wide, flat rock. It was all achingly familiar.

"Hello," she whispered. "It's me, Amy. Aren't you there?"

She sat for a while, not sure what else to do, until the shadows got longer. As the last shaft of sunlight fell between two trees, lighting a patch of the pond, she saw something shining in the water. She took off her shoes and pulled her dress up, not wanting the material to get wet.

The pebbles under her feet were slippery, so she tried to walk on the sand in between. It squished, all slimy and soft between her toes, making her giggle. She got to the shiny thing and, balancing carefully, put one hand into the water. She had to dig into the sand to prise it up, it was so smooth.

It came free and she pulled it to the surface. The golden acorn was small enough to fit in the palm of her hand. Turning it between her fingers, the hem of her forgotten dress flirting with the water, she saw that one side of it was cracked and open, revealing a red jewel that looked at her, like an unblinking eye.

The glen had gone quiet. Too quiet. Even Mark's splashes had stopped. Spooked by the silence and the growing darkness, she began to wade back, slipping and sliding. She'd barely made it to the edge of the pool when the music started: the same music she'd danced to last year. Bubbles came into her stomach, fizzing with promise. She forgot about the darkness. She turned and splashed back through the pond to the far side, pushing back overhanging branches that closed behind her.

She found herself in a bigger glen, one that hadn't been there the year before. A fairy appeared in front of her, about her own age, pretty-faced with sugar-pink wings and a sparkly wand, as if from a storybook. The fairy took her hand, its fingers feathery, and Amy danced forwards. Fairies filled the glen and she was passed from one soft hand to another, spinning and happy. A smell reached her, of berries and apples, summer pressed into a bottle.

She reached the glen's centre, where the most lovely woman she'd ever seen stood, her golden hair in ringlets and a gentle smile in place. A pair of wings were folded behind her, making her seem even taller.

Amy bowed, somehow knowing that was what to do. The Queen – it had to be, she had a crown and a fairy wand – stepped from the stone she'd been standing on. She held her hand out, palm up.

Amy backed away, suddenly uncertain. The Queen's

face changed. Her smile vanished and her eyes narrowed. The music became broken, as if all the notes were in the wrong place. The dancing stopped. The Queen towered over Amy, and there were other fairies on her shoulders – small with dark, sharp eyes.

The queen reached for Amy, who shrank back further. The acorn in her hand grew warm, like a warning. She remembered that her dad and Mark were waiting for her back in the glen, and she wanted nothing more than to be back with them.

She ran for the pond, squirming past hands that grabbed at her. The fairies weren't pretty now, but twisted, all broken noses and dark eyes. The smell of the glen changed to something dark and old: the stench of rotting leaves in the winter; of a still, dead pool.

She continued to run, but still couldn't see the pool. She'd tell Mum and Dad that she'd been wrong and she didn't want to spend the week here. She'd tell them she never wanted to come back.

"Amy!" The voice was familiar. She ran to it, hands out. "Wake up. You're going to have the whole house up."

Her eyes flew open. Mark was sitting up in the second bed.

"You all right?" he asked. Even in the darkness she could hear the strain in his casual voice – it held an edge, a rising at the end of the question that told her she'd frightened him. Again. Once more. Forever.

Slowly, she nodded. She hadn't remembered running from the glen before. The rest of it, the acorn, the Queen, was familiar. She'd had that dream through most of her life, so often she didn't know how much of it came from her five-year-old self lost in the glen, or had been added to through the years. But the fear, the scratching hands….that was new.

"Sorry," she said, and she was. Sorry she'd had it, sorry he'd heard it, sorry she didn't know the truth from a lie.

"Want to talk about it?" He sounded drained. A clock glowed on the table between them, showing half past three.

"No." She lay down, forcing herself not to shake. It wasn't fair, keeping him up. "It was just a dream."

He settled, his breathing turning back to the steadiness of earlier. She hardly dared to close her eyes. She didn't want to remember the terror of being five and lost. She clutched the acorn in her right hand, letting its hard edges dig into her palm. It had come with her, through the flight from the glen. Somehow she had made it back that time. It had kept her safe then, as it had done ever since.

She needed it to. The fairies who had lured her to the waterfall tonight were the ones of her dream. Fairies with sharp nails that had torn her skin, who'd hissed hatred when she'd seen Mark's torch and ran to the light. She hadn't understood how they could be so different from any she'd heard before. Now she knew they weren't different; she'd just forgotten.

Chapter Seven

S UNLIGHT STREAMED THROUGH the bay window of the breakfast room, changing the landscape from the previous night's sinister place. The farmhouse next to the B&B was bathed in the sunlight, looking like something that belonged on a postcard. Simon stretched his leg and flexed his ankle. The night's sleep had helped, leaving only the odd twinge. Between that and the Ulster fry from hell he felt vaguely human, and the memories of the night before were more in perspective. There had been no gripping hands, no eyes watching him, just a confused girl caught up in the atmosphere of an eerie place. As if sensing his thoughts, Amy, across the table, gave him a quick smile. She looked as though she'd had even less sleep than him.

He drained the last of his coffee. As if by magic May appeared, wielding the pot like a kitchen ninja. The smell of the coffee drifted up – nirvana, that's what it was – and he took a sip. Industrial strength didn't even begin to describe it.

"So," he said, his voice forced, "what are your plans?"

"Get back to Belfast, I suppose," said Mark. He had laid the sugar sachets in a row and kept rearranging them, his fingers quick and distracting. "Drop Amy off with Mum."

"Tell her nothing," urged Amy. "Really, I'll never hear the end of it."

"I can't – I already said you had a turn."

"Tell her I threw up, and that's what you meant." She fidgeted in her seat. "Please, Mark. You don't know what she's like. Don't tell her I—"

Simon leaned forward, despite himself. *She what?* Ran off chasing fairies? Or did she have a different name for it?

"Got a bit distracted," she offered, eventually.

Mark's face twisted. "Right. That will get her off your scent." He pointed one of the sugar packets at her. "You were freaking out before she left. She'll know."

"Not if you don't tell." She rolled her eyes. "If you tell I'll have weeks of describing what the fairies sounded like, and what they said. It's like living with the Gestapo."

"At least she lets you stay," said Mark, and his words were sour. "The Gestapo's better than the two-room shithole I'm in."

May bustled in and out of the kitchen, setting jams on the sideboard, and cleaning surfaces. Simon reckoned she had more than a half ear on the conversation. Mark rubbed his forehead and gave a resigned nod to his sister.

"All right," he said. "I'll cover for you." His voice was bitter. "Again."

The landlady stopped, obviously not sure if she should intervene, and Simon offered her his best smile. It wasn't her fault she'd ended up stuck with the neighbourhood kooky family.

"That breakfast was smashing. I feel like a new man."

A supporting murmur from Mark and Amy made May beam. "Best breakfast in the glens. Check out TripAdvisor; number two of fifteen we are." She frowned, as if contemplating what it would take to get to number one. "All *my* comments mention the breakfast."

"I'll make sure to add one. Best hangover cure, will that do?" said Simon. She pursed her lips. Maybe not. He finished his coffee and pushed his chair back. "Tell me this – getting back to Belfast, do you have public transport out here at the weekend?" He'd have googled it but his smartphone lay on the table, dead and useless, with no reception at all.

"Of course. After breakfast, I'll give you a lift to the village." May busied herself with clearing the table. "Did you sleep well? My rooms often get a mention, too."

"Great, thanks," said Mark.

"Like a log." Simon kept his face bland. "I was knackered."

May eyed him shrewdly. "Did you see anything in the glen last night?" She lowered her voice. "They say the wee folk are there."

Wee folk? What was this: *Fairy-tales of Ireland*? Amy poured herself a cup of tea and lifted it, her hands hugged around it. Mark's eyes narrowed. Simon took another gulp of his coffee. "There's no such thing."

"Ah, now." May pulled a chair out and his heart sank; she had the glazed look of an expert, one who would happily talk for hours. "That's dangerous talk. *They* like to be believed in." She glanced over her shoulder, towards the kitchen, and it made him wonder if she believed so much she left out milk for the fairies at night. Somehow, in this landscape, he wouldn't actually blame her.

"In the glen where you were, you get leprechauns." She

looked completely serious. "But up on the top of the ridge – there, you get the pooka. They're a different matter: they're shape-changers, and they're deadly bad spirits. They can be anything – horses, or eagles. Anything at all, and you wouldn't know until they were right on top of you."

Simon glanced across at Amy. She looked sick. Or scared. Maybe both. He noticed for the first time she had her pendant back on, tied with a thin string of red ribbon.

"Aye, well, there were no eagles around last night," he said. There hadn't been *anything* last night, other than the wind. "A couple of owls – are they anything to be worried about?"

May tapped his hand. "You shouldn't dismiss it. There're others: the watershee and the banshee and the changelings."

Amy made a small noise, which might have been a cough or a snort, and Mark got to his feet, so quickly his chair nearly toppled. "Can I see those timetables?" He was too terse: another lightning change of mood that he seemed prone to.

May followed him out to the hall, her back straight and offended. Silence stretched between Simon and Amy. A noise, soft but insistent, grew. Simon looked around, trying to locate it, and his gaze fell on Amy's arm. She was scratching so hard tendrils of blood crept down and traced the fine bones of her wrist. *Oh, Jesus, she wasn't right in the head.* He reached out and put his hand over hers, drawing it away from her arm and onto the table.

"Don't hurt yourself." He nodded at the door. "And don't let her annoy you. It's just… stories. Stories from a part of the world cut off from anywhere for years, where they still have different ways. I know you got a bit drunk yesterday, and you had notions, but there's nothing—"

"I wasn't drunk. I don't drink – I'm on medication." She pulled her hand away. "I know I sound crazy, but I'm not. All those things that lady said – they talk to me." She paused. "Except the pooka. Thank God, I don't like the sound of that one."

Her eyes searched his, dark and huge. She was serious. He took in her scratched arms and scared eyes and he wanted to take away her fear. There had to be a way to make her see what she believed couldn't be true. A way to make her smile again, the way she had when she'd talked about the speeches. He'd got a laugh then, maybe he could again. But she looked as far away from laughing as anyone he'd even seen. Whoever it was that might put Amy Lyle back on her feet, it wasn't him.

He stood, feeling useless. "I'll have to get the next bus. I need to get back to town."

"Of course you do." She smiled, but it was sad around the edges.

What would happen next time the voices came? Would she end up somewhere more dangerous than the glen last night? He wished he could find something helpful to say. Knowing him, he'd make things worse. He stepped away but still her gaze held his. A hard lump swelled in his throat. He couldn't just leave it on this hopeless note.

"So…" He paused; what *should* he say? Tell her she was a liar or pretend to believe? He cleared his throat. Anything had to be better than standing in silence. "Maybe you've got this thing with the voices the wrong way round."

"What?"

"It doesn't matter that they called you. It only matters that you answered."

She grabbed her bag and got up, moving gracefully around the table. If he'd done the same, he'd have knocked over the table or the chair. The light from the window streamed behind her, making a halo. Her eyes met his again, fey and watchful. She was tense, almost on the balls of her feet, her bag pulled across her body so tightly it pulled her dress out of shape. "You don't know what it's like."

"So tell me."

"I can't." A shadow crossed the sun, breaking the halo's spell, and he stepped back. How could she believe the voices and seem so normal? How could she be both the biggest thing in the room and the smallest?

"Look, I know you've a few things going on," he said, "but maybe you need to find a way to say no." Something had to get through to her. "Maybe you need to confront whatever it is: the voices, the fairies, I don't know, and tell them to piss off."

"Tell them to piss off?"

He couldn't tell if she was astonished or angry. "Yeah." He put everything he had into making the words sound sincere. "When are they strongest?"

She cocked her head. Was she listening to him or something else, something he had no way of hearing or seeing?

"It's not when, it's where," she said at last. Her shoulders rose and fell with a deep, shuddering breath. "By the lakes and the rivers. In the countryside. Not so much in the city. Although the bloody leprechauns would get in where a draught wouldn't. And don't start me on the urban elves…" She bit her lip. "But it's never been like it was yesterday: so real, so loud, as if they were actually close to me. And then later…." She looked towards the glen. "Later, they *were* real. I could touch them. My mother says I've always been fey and that's why they come to me." She screwed her face up. "That's some of what she says, anyway."

Her mother was right. In the forest she'd been so much part of the landscape, it had been as if she'd been dropped in from a fairytale. He found himself staring at her, taking in the hollow of her neck; the pendant lying against her skin; the cut of her hair, close, almost elfin; the way she stood, alert and tense. He tried to work out which was the real Amy – this one, earnest and honest, or the fey girl called by the trees in the glen.

Her hand came up to her throat and fiddled with her necklace, turning the acorn round and round so he could see one side of it was broken.

"Yesterday... from the moment I got there, all the way through the speeches, the voices were whispering my name, calling me." Her cheeks flushed. "God, this sounds so stupid. Anyway, I *tried* not to listen. I thought they'd go away, like they always do."

Her eyes pleaded for understanding. *Oh, God, what a way to live.* What she was saying sounded mad, completely off-beat, but she obviously believed it. Either that, or it was a way of getting attention. She certainly had her brother at her beck and call and, from the sound of it, her mother too.

"Well maybe you should go and find the urban elves, or the shee, or whatever there is, and say you're not coming back." He paused, but she didn't seem angry, so he pushed on. "There must be somewhere you can go. I mean, they don't follow you to the toilet, do they?"

She gave a small smile. "No." She bit her lip, an eye-tooth worrying at it. "Well, not often." If she was putting this on, it was the best show he'd seen in years. Her eyes widened, as if she'd just realised something. "There is one place where they didn't bother me. It's been years since I've been there – I'd forgotten."

"Where?" This was important; if she believed there was somewhere safe, maybe she could carry that safety to other places. He found himself moving closer, wanting to convince her. "Safe is good."

"My dad sailed to some sea-caves on the North coast. He lives on his boat, see, and he took me and Mark with him for a holiday. They were exactly the sort of place the fairies would be, but they were quiet." She ducked her head, as if embarrassed, and turned away a little. "I've always thought I'd like to go back but I've never dared. In case it's changed."

He wanted her to face him. He wanted to take her hand and tell her it would be okay, that it wouldn't always be as bad as yesterday. He wanted to take the bus up the coast to find the sea caves where she was safe. He could see the curve of her shoulder, her head ducked towards it. Something turned over in his stomach, making his breath catch.

A clock chimed in the hall, breaking the moment. In a minute or two, May would bustle in to give him a lift.

"Well, look, good luck," he said. What use would it do, taking her up the coast? Knowing his luck, they'd get to the caves and she'd imagine them crawling with fairies. That would do more damage than anything. "And... no more midnight rambling, eh?"

"Okay." She gave a low laugh and it was all he could do to start walking towards the hall. He got halfway before he turned back, cursing himself.

"If you want to chat anytime, give me a ring." He managed a smile, but could hear his ma's voice in his ear – 'another waif, Simon, another mercy mission? You still have the kitten from down the road in residence'. He pulled out one of the business cards he'd brought to hand around at the wedding to show Simon McCormick wasn't the thick eejit everyone thought. He gave it to Amy. "It might be nice to have a coffee sometime."

"You have your own business?" she said.

"I just set up websites." He smiled, not able to resist a tease. "I could do you one; fairy-finder for hire?"

She laughed, a proper laugh and he felt ridiculously pleased with himself. Then she glanced out of the window and her face sobered. She seemed to shrink in on herself, becoming a whip of a girl facing a world of demons again.

His smile fell away. Whatever problems Amy Lyle fought, with his talent for putting his foot in it, he'd fuck things up worse. Just ask his dad. Amy didn't need someone cack-handed like him. He left the dining room and this time didn't look back.

CHAPTER EIGHT

A MY WATCHED SIMON pace into the hall, leaving her alone. He must think she was crazy, even though he'd been nice about it. How had he put it again? That she had a few things going on. She clutched his business card and smiled. Anyone could have things going on.

Amy. The whisper cut through the silence. She tensed, coming onto the balls of her feet, the familiar fight-or-flight coursing through her. Not now, not today. Surely the fairies could feel her just as clearly as she them? *I'm too tired.* She wanted to curl up on a bus and sleep her way out of the glens.

She clenched her bag against her, as if it could fend the voices off and tried to think of anything that might hold them at bay. She couldn't spend another day like yesterday. *Amy, Amy, Amy...* Sing-song on the surface, but with sharp determination underneath.

"No." She closed her eyes but the voices were circling her, calling her name again and again. A sob caught in her throat.

She had the think of something other than the voices. Desperately, she searched through her memories. Simon's touch as he'd washed her feet and treated her like something precious; Mark's quiet watchfulness, his determination to keep her where she should be. Still, the voices came.

She clenched her fists, letting her nails dig into her palms, and the pain helped her stay grounded in what was real. She reminded herself that she was in a public place, with her brother upstairs collecting their things and a nice bloke who'd pretended she wasn't mad standing on the porch, where she could see his outline through the window. Nothing could happen here, in this room. Nothing at all.

Amy, Amy, Amy.

"Go away. I'm not listening." But she didn't move. Damn it; damn them, they *knew* she was listening. She *always* listened. Her palms grew clammy. She tried to breathe deeply, counting to four slowly, holding it, and then out. Her panic receded, and she opened her eyes.

A tractor worked in the field opposite, making its way around a tree in the centre of the field. A fairy-thorn, not to be touched for fear of the fairies' wrath. The local people believed the fairies were real. They had no doubt this land was linked to the fae.

A flash of sun glinted off the tractor's roof and caught her eyes, making candy canes stripe her vision in the unmistakeable start of an aura migraine. *Not now*, she thought fiercely. But of course it was now: she was tired, she was stressed, and there'd been thunder in the air since yesterday. Migraines crept through any hole of opportunity.

The carpet wavered, making her uncertain of her footing. She couldn't move in case she fell. She put her hand out to steady herself on the sideboard. The aura danced.

Come to us, dance with us.

She tightened her grip on the sideboard's lipped surface. She wasn't going. Last night – the music, the dancing, the singing – couldn't have been real. Except the blisters on her feet were real, as if she *had* danced for hours.

Amy, Amy, Amy. The voices sharpened. She jerked her chin in defiance. She could wait them out. She'd managed to hold them off all day yesterday. Even when she'd tried to go up to the waterfall and Simon had stopped her, she'd managed – just – to turn away. She'd held on, right to the moment the band stopped and the lights had come up in the comparative silence. The voices had seized that silence and blasted her – but until that moment, she hadn't fallen.

Something knocked against the window, wings fluttering. A butterfly, she told herself, but the butterfly had a pointed face and smile that revealed sharp teeth. It had to be the migraine. She clung to that thought, keeping it strong.

The fairy batted the window. Its mouth drew back. *Come with us.* The fairy's words were drawn out, lengthened in warning. Amy's breath caught. The fairy gave an awful grin, teeth glistening through blood-red lips. *We need you.*

Amy shook her head. Her hand went to her necklace. She gripped it so tightly the detail of the acorn dug into her.

"Go away," she murmured. "I'm not answering." She didn't dare. To succumb again would lead her to their world. She tightened her fingers, so that the string stretched and dug into the back of her neck. Her only chance was to get out of the B&B with Mark and get to Belfast. Once there, she'd seek help. She'd admit herself, if that was needed, and see every therapist until the voices were gone this time, once and for all, and she wouldn't be sidetracked.

"Can you hear me?" she said to the empty room. She planted her feet and faced the window. "I will not let you ruin my life. I will not."

Liar, liar. The words came not just from the fairy fluttering by the window, but from the hills around the cottage, through the trees, carried in the wind, a cacophony that dazed her. She put her hands up, pulling at her hair. It was impossible to distract herself from this. The business card fell from her grasp as she staggered to the breakfast table. *Liar, liar, liar…*

"No." Her voice was a moan. She bent for Simon's card, scrabbling for it, not knowing why she couldn't let it go, just that he'd been the only thing normal yesterday in the glen. He'd held her back – perhaps by keeping his card she could hold firm today. She closed her fingers around it. Fairy-hunter; he had no idea how right he was. She could find them anywhere. Or they found her; she didn't know which.

Still the voices came. The tree on the hill appeared and vanished in the aura, at once there, then gone. This place was no good; too close to them. She had to get out before the fairies wore her down. In the glen, she'd begged them to stop dancing but they'd forced her to her feet. She'd danced until her sandal came loose but had kept going. She'd danced, twirling and turning, until she'd been lost in the dark, on the edge of their world. Without Mark's light, she wouldn't have come back. She'd already dropped her acorn, and she knew not to do that.

Terror crept up her spine, chilling her blood, the sure knowledge she had no defences. Not here, so close to where they dwelt.

Come, come, come. She walked to the kitchen, her steps

numbed and slow. They knew she planned to leave – and that, once gone from this land, so infected with the fairies, she'd never come back. They would not give her that chance. The voices sighed their support. In a dream, she reached for the back door. Her bag slid from her shoulder, onto the floor, and she didn't try to stop it. She wouldn't need it wherever she was going.

A spike of fear almost broke through their hold, but her hand was already closing on the doorknob. She tried not to open it, to fight the voices and the fear rising in her. She could choose to stay. She *could*.

She couldn't, though. She wrenched the door open and stepped out into the late morning sunshine. The farmyard stretched to the glen beyond. Another fairy-thorn crowned the hill.

The fairy voices grew louder, encouraging her forwards. She managed a last look over her shoulder at the kitchen door, creaking as it rocked back and forth, back and forth. She hoped Simon would come out, or Mark, but no one did. She turned away and set off across the farmyard, following the voices she couldn't deny.

CHAPTER NINE

SIMON WAITED IN the porch of the guesthouse. A low bookcase spanned one wall, the books – mostly from bookclubs – curling in the damp air. Beside it, a haphazard box of toys sat gathering cobwebs, presumably for the summer season when families might visit the coast. A detailed map of the nearest town hung on the opposite wall and he scanned it, trying to place the B&B. The town was a dot on the road. The sooner he got away, the better.

May's car pulled up in front of the porch, and she got out, keys in hand. "I'll clear the back seat. Everyone ready?"

Simon moved quickly to the foot of the stairs. "We're going!"

"Right." Mark appeared at the top. "Where's Amy?"

"Still in the breakfast room."

Mark thumped down the stairs and stuck his head around the door. "Amy, come on!" After a moment of no answer he padded into the room. "Amy, let's go."

A worm of worry started, low in Simon's stomach. He found himself glancing out of the open front door. The glen loomed over the house, the road a bare ribbon separating him from it.

Mark came back out to the hall, a frown on his face. "You're sure she didn't go outside?"

Not again. Simon shook his head. "I've been here the whole time." Waiting, he realised. Keeping an eye out for her? Or watching for anything moving outside? Either the place or Amy had put thoughts into his head.

Mark turned to May. "Any other way out?" His voice held the edge of panic. Last night Simon hadn't understood why, but now he knew exactly what Mark was thinking: if she'd bolted in this bare landscape, they might never find her. His throat tightened. If they didn't find her, where would she go? To the voices? Where would they lead her if she did? In crazed circles on the hillside? Back to the glen?

"Through the kitchen." May was already on her way, Mark behind her. Simon followed, glad to be moving, through the breakfast room and into the kitchen. Amy's bag lay on the floor, its flap open, a packet of pills threatening to spill out. The back door swung lightly to and fro. Simon swore under his breath.

"Oh, for fuck's sake," said Mark, the soul of eloquence.

May looked appalled and Simon touched her elbow. "He's worried, he didn't mean it."

He followed Mark to the back door and scanned the sparse hillside beyond the farmyard. Field after field of grass, hedgerows and sheep, but no sign of Amy. A lane to the left of the yard snaked along the bank of a river; a second fork ran behind the farmhouse and up to the ridge.

He stepped outside, shivering in the chill air. The farm was bigger than it had seemed in the dark. Three long barns ranged at the top end of the yard, rusted machinery and a woodpile leaned against them. A low fence ringed the yard off from the surrounding hills. He stared around, helpless. She could be anywhere.

Mark's dark eyes were hard to read. "Amy!" The words echoed off the hill. He ran his hands through his hair. "We have to find her before she gets worse."

"Worse?" She got worse than this? The horizon darkened, a line of grey on green, and the air smelt heavy with expectant rain.

"Sicker," clarified Mark. "She has episodes – she's been in and out of mental institutions half her life."

That was what his ma had said: Amy Lyle was away with the wee birds. He hadn't taken it in at the time – Ma often claimed people weren't right in the head and the scourge of their mothers' lives. She said it about him at least once a week. Last night, when Amy had told him about the voices, it had sounded more kooky than dangerous. But to have taken her to a mental ward... he scanned the hill again, quicker, his hand over his eyes.

"So, when she gets back the doctors can help her?" Surely they must be able to help her.

"Not easily." Mark's hand clenched on the wood of the fence. "They won't even say what's wrong. Some sort of schizophrenia, perhaps." He gave a short, humourless laugh. "Trust me, she doesn't hear fairies, she's *away* with them." He pushed off from the fence. "And she's out there, on her own, without her tablets. Let's get looking."

May grabbed his arm. "Shall I call the police?"

"They probably won't do anything." Mark looked a little embarrassed. "I've dealt with them before. She hasn't been missing long enough." The top of the ridge had vanished into the dark clouds, its tree a dull smudge. "It's better we just find her."

"You check the right lane and I'll head up to the ridge," said Simon. He couldn't tell if he was avoiding the path along the river through denial, or cowardice. "She can't have gone far."

"Let's hope not." Mark set off at a jog, calling his sister's name.

"I'll take the car along the main road," said May. Her face was hard to read, but her eyes were sharp; she'd missed nothing of the conversation.

Simon hurried into the lane, ignoring a twinge of protest from his ankle, and followed the hedgerow, watching for any movement or flash of colour. If she was around she should be visible in such a bleak landscape. His feet slipped in mud, but he kept going, determined to carry out his part of the search thoroughly. As Mark had said, the quicker she was found, the better. Then he'd get the hell out of here. He was done chasing her up hills.

"Amy!" Nothing but the wind through the hedgerows. "Amy!" A brutal gust swept across the lane and he had to stop and plant his feet. He glanced back at the guesthouse; he'd come further than he'd expected. The sky had filled with black clouds. She wouldn't stay out when the storm hit, surely? He was tempted to head back, but a freezing wind caught him, cold for an early autumn day, and he didn't have it in him to leave her out there alone. He climbed a metal-barred gate, set into a break in the hedgerow, and jumped down, into a field above the farmhouse. His ankle complained more earnestly, but he put that from his mind and set off, calling for her as he went.

CHAPTER TEN

A DOG SNARLED, making Amy stop, her heart beating too hard. She'd reached a second fence that marked the very edge of the farm, one foot in front of the other. Shouts had come from the farmhouse, combining with the fairies calling her name, but she'd ignored them. Mark, she supposed, and Simon. They'd be looking for her. If so, they hadn't come this way.

A second snarl came, low and threatening. The dog padded into sight, a scraggly collie-type, roving along the fence as if corralling her. A barred gate, giving access to the hill beyond, could easily be cut off by the dog. To her left, a hedgerow separated the yard from a lane. Its branches twisted in the wind, leaves rustling. She tried to push her way through, but the branches were too densely packed. A whisper came, calling her up the hill and a shadow detached itself from the undergrowth and crept across the yard, long fingers of menace reaching for the dog. It crouched low, hackles raised, eyes seeking what it could sense but not attack.

Ours, the shadow seemed to say. *She's ours.* Amy straightened, fists clenched. She didn't want to be anyone's. The air grew cold.

The dog held its ground. The shadow reached for it over ripples of mud and the dog yelped. Tail down, at last it ran, so fast its legs flashed beneath it. The shadow raced after it until, with a long yelp, the animal fell, legs twitching. Its eyes rolled back, white and motionless.

Amy stumbled away as the shadow passed her, drawing back into the hedgerow. The dog didn't move.

Come, come, come. The words were as cold as the air. She could feel the sense of the shadow, as if it were watching her. Quickly, she climbed the gate and joined a ragged trail, which rose steeply to the ridge.

A single voice came from the brow of the hill, singing a song of long, low notes that drew her forwards. Another joined it, calling her name. The farmhouse fell behind her. A knot of fear wound tight in her stomach. It didn't matter that she didn't know the way – the land would guide her. Just like it had shown her the way to the ridge. Her mother had been right all along: she belonged here.

The hill grew steeper. The shadow returned, keeping pace just at the edge of her vision. When she turned her head it disappeared, only to reform again once she looked away.

Her steps slowed. The hill was bleak, the wind raw. What heat there had been from the sun was gone. Rain started, a ferocious downpour that quickly soaked Amy to her skin. A smell rose from the ground, heavy and cloying. Her breath came in quick gasps, her chest rising and falling. The smell grew stronger.

Someone's old, cold breath, close to her; someone watching her. She shuddered. Puddles pooled on the path, reflecting the dark sky and scudding clouds. The sense of breathing circled her. Something touched her behind the ear, on the back of her neck. She didn't dare look behind. To look would be to know this was real, not a voice that could be dismissed. She strained her ears for the sound of movement, for the whisper of a word, but there was only the noise of the pouring rain. She opened her mouth to say no, to plead for her freedom, but no words came out.

"Amy!" The voice carried over the hillside, ebbing with the wind. "Amy!"

She brought her head up. "Mark?" Or Simon. One of them, for sure. She pushed away her fear and ran towards the voices, seeking them. The shadow rose from the hedgerow, growing in height and breath, blocking her path. She stopped. Images of the dog came to her: its dead eyes, its last long yelp.

*Amy, come to us, come to us...*The voices were stronger than ever. Whatever they'd found in her, they wanted it. She lifted a foot. She didn't want to go. Sing, she told herself. If she was singing, she wasn't listening.

She sang off-key, like her dad. He used to say it wasn't that Amy couldn't sing, it was that she copied him too well. Need for her dad – drunk, maudlin, but preferably sober – made her gasp. The shadow drew back. Hope filled her, that she'd find a way to get past it, that she'd be safe if she kept singing.

If she got to the bottom of the hill, she could get a taxi to Dad's boat. He'd make sure she was all right – he practically kept her on a tether when she visited, even sleeping on the bottom step in case she tried to get out. Once she slept, she'd be okay.

She took a step down the hill, and then another. It was easier now she'd started.

The voices grew louder. *Come, come, come.* The shadow reached for her, its long fingers sinking into her skin, bringing a cold like she had never felt before, one that leeched into her bones. Her teeth were chattering. She forgot the next word. Her steps faltered.

A screech came from above, angry and hard. A black shape raced across the hill opposite, darkness on darkness. *The pooka.* Fear trapped her. The shadow wreathed her, and she didn't stop it. It forced her to a metal stile set in the hedgerow.

A green tourist sign proclaimed the name Oisin's grave. Her breath caught. Enchanted Oisin, who had fallen from his horse and died, mortal, never to return to Tir-na-nog. Hands formed at the small of her back, a multitude of fingers, and pushed her over the stile into a field, bleak and sparse, more rocks than grass.

In its centre, a stone circle lay scattered on the hillside, as if some giant's hand had dropped it. A sense of something old – *sly* – came from the circle. Cold tendrils curled around her legs, climbing to her waist.

The hands shoved her forwards. She staggered and put her hand to her throat and grasped her acorn, holding it tight and close. She would not drop it this time. She would not dare to.

She passed a small cairn in the lee of the hedgerow, a mountain ash growing from its peak, a small plaque shining through the grass. *John Hewitt. My chosen ground.*

John Hewitt, the poet of the glens. It made sense now, why she was here. A poet and a mythical hero's last place: the site was enchanted. She didn't have time to take the thought further; already the hands were on her again. They forced her to the stones, standing sharp against the bare field.

A tangled cluster of three knee-high rocks, grass-choked, formed around a gap the size of her fist. She reached for the gap, hands shaking. It was here; the join between this world and the other. It tugged at her; called to her. The gap grew, at first big enough to crawl into, then large enough to walk through.

Her acorn grew hot against her throat. She lifted it and the ribbon dug into her neck. One pull and it would be free. Like it had been last night. The knot dug into the back of her neck, the string growing thin and weak until it snapped: the acorn came free, unfettered. She put her head back, Amy and not-Amy, scared and exultant; at peace and arrow-tense.

She reached out her hand, the acorn squeezed painfully between the tips of her index finger and thumb, and touched the golden pendant to the portal. A blast of wind swirled around her, whistling, spinning.

Shapes formed in front of her, emerging from the hole. One came right up to her face – a fairy, its hair in soft ringlets, its wings beating in steady rhythm. More formed up, as if an army: elves and sprites, the size of her forearms; a troop of twisted brownies, stooped and wizened with dark, hard eyes.

Now, said a voice, deep and old. The Shadow. Her legs trembled as she stepped forward. Fairies covered her arms, clung to her hair. More danced before her, leading her onwards.

She opened the hand that held the acorn. It had got her out of a fairy glen when she was five; now it would take her back to them. No brother would rescue her. No kind bloke would stop her going further. Once she dropped the acorn into the tangled portal, there would be no return.

Beyond, the fairy world took shape, greener than any land she'd seen. The sky, a deepest turquoise, contrasted with the darkness that surrounded her. Music carried from it, a mournful song that spoke of loss. It sped, promising happiness. She recognised the music from the waterfall. She'd danced to it for hours. Death and life, sadness and joy; each the opposite of the other.

Her mouth moistened with need. She didn't care about the danger. The fairy-world sharpened: a green expanse led to a golden throne where a lady waited, her kind face and eyes crowned in gold. Amy knew her; she'd met her before.

She opened her hand and held the acorn out. She dropped into a curtsey. "My Queen."

"Amy!" The voice was no fairy's voice – it had the harsh edge of a Belfast accent. She pulled her hand back.

Mine. The Queen got to her feet, graceful even when hurried. Her face twisted, no longer friendly.

"Amy! Thank God you're all right." Twenty yards or so behind the fairyland, Simon crested the brow of the hill, a strained smile in place. "We've been looking for you."

Amy backed away from the queen. The stone portal shrank back to a gap between three misplaced stones. There was no throne, no sky, just a cobweb-filled space.

She shivered, for the first time noticing how the rain had soaked through her dress, but got to her feet.

Leave him. She'd never heard so much hatred in a voice. Hatred that was insistent and unassailable. The Queen's, whom all fairies must obey. *You're ours.* Amy couldn't stay here. Not on her own, not with Simon, not at all.

She ran, away from Simon, not daring to pass the stone circle. A shadow broke from the hedgerow and she veered away from the stile, angling up the field. Simon shouted her name, but she didn't turn back – she didn't dare. She jumped the low fence into the next field, yelling as it caught her leg. She kept running, up and up. She couldn't go back to the circle; she could only go forwards.

"HELL!" SIMON HURRIED to the stone circle. His ankle hampered him, complaining at the hill's incline. By the time he reached it, she was gone.

He slowed to a halt, taking his time to scan the hill and hedgerows but Amy had disappeared over the brow of the hill. The singing he'd followed, ebbing and flowing clearly despite the harsh rain, had gone, too. He put his hand in his pocket for his phone – there were people better qualified to look for her; it was time they were involved. At least they'd know where to start a search. His hand clenched around nothing, and he remembered with a start that he'd set it down in the dining room, disgusted at the lack of signal.

A mist descended, thick and fast, even for a hillside. Within minutes he could barely see two feet ahead. The grass faded, washed in grey, but he wasn't far from the farm and, for all the place was remote, there was a road close by and a village not three miles away.

Something shifted against his cheek, a breeze that shouldn't be, not in such a heavy, dank mist. He swiped at the air and sped up, stumbling, blind, half-tripping on a rabbit hole. He walked for too long. Shadows appeared and disappeared in the greyness but he kept going, not willing to admit he'd got lost. The first rule of a search, he remembered from his scouting days. Don't become a problem yourself. He'd gone and broken it.

The rain came again, breaking the mist enough to see. He was in a field, no path in sight, no road anywhere near him, nothing but pissing rain. He hoped Mark had called the police and got someone searching; he didn't want to spend the night out in this. For now, he stumbled on, hoping to catch sight of the road, or the farm or, at the very least, find somewhere to shelter. And all the time, there was no sign of Amy; once again, she'd vanished like a wraith.

CHAPTER ELEVEN

MARK GLANCED AT the clock on the wall of the lounge. Another half an hour had passed since he'd last checked. Worry settled, deep in his stomach, and the silence in the room wasn't helping. There had been no sightings of Amy by any of the neighbours May had contacted, and none of Simon either. At this rate his mum, called an hour ago and on her way, would get to the farmhouse first.

"Right." May sounded calm and in control, as she had been the whole morning. "It's time to call the police." She nodded out the window. "Especially with that weather. If I'm any judge, the storm's only just started."

"They might not do anything. She hasn't been missing long enough." It had been hard to get the police interested when Amy was a teenager. As an adult, and one who'd run voluntarily, it would be even harder.

May looked scandalised. "In these parts, they'll do something if they're asked by someone sensible." She picked up the phone and he didn't stop her. She might be right – it was one thing for Amy to go walkabout in Belfast, where there were plenty of people about and she knew her way home. Here, the police might well be more helpful. "We need this wee girl found, and we need a proper amount of bodies looking to do that." She didn't mention the scale of the search, nor needles in haystacks, thankfully.

The crunch of a car turning into the driveway interrupted her and she cut the call before it had been answered. Mark crossed to the window. His mum's car had pulled up in front of the house and, to his amazement, both his parents appeared. That Mum had called his father was astonishing; that he'd been sober enough to come along was nearly a miracle.

His mum raised a hand in greeting and even through rain he could see her pursed lips. She looked half the woman she'd been the night before, a haunted shadow he knew from the past. He hurried to the door.

"Mark!" His dad stepped forward, hair tied back with what looked to be one of the red elastic bands postmen dropped. His fisherman's jumper had, as ever, holes within the holes. He must have come straight from the boat: he smelled of diesel and brine, familiar from Mark's childhood visits, learning how to work the ropes and handle an outboard. God only knew what staid, clean-living May would make of him.

It didn't matter; when he took Mark's arm he felt solid, and Mark was relieved he had come: even a piss-head of a father was better than an absent one.

"Any sign of her?" asked his dad.

"She can't be far." May bustled past Mark. "I have the local farmers watching for her, and I've just spoken to the police. They're on their way."

Mum stepped forward, her eyes flinty. "I think calling

the police is a little premature."

Mark stared. Mum knew Amy wasn't well – she'd noticed at the wedding yesterday. She should be beating down the door of the police station. Anytime Amy had gone off in the past, Mum had shouted loudest, and longest, for something to be done. He exchanged a glance with his dad who gave a brief, confused shrug.

"Not a bit of it," said May. "It'll take time to get a search underway. We need people out there, before it's dark." She pushed the door wide. "Now, come in. It's been a shock, I'm sure."

She led them down a short corridor beyond the breakfast room to a formal sitting-room, no doubt kept for best. Mark perched on the windowsill looking over the farmyard, as far from his parents as he could; the atmosphere was sharp enough to cut.

An awkward silence fell. Mum radiated anger, directed at him he was sure, and with good reason – he should have known better than to leave Amy in the breakfast room this morning. He looked away, not able to face the pinched look.

His dad's hands were clasped together, presumably to stop them shaking. He stared firmly ahead but, after a moment, stole a glance at a sideboard display of three decanters. They must have been purely for show: the contents were dark and the stoppers covered in a fine film of dust. That wasn't putting Dad off, judging by the hungry look in his eyes.

At the sound of the front door opening, Dad tore his eyes away, a thin line of sweat along his brow. Voices carried from the hallway, and the sound of footsteps. Two police officers, a man and a woman, came into the room.

The policewoman gave a firm nod. "Thanks, May. We'll take it from here."

May left, closing the door behind her, but Mark fancied an even bet she was outside listening.

"It's your daughter who is missing, yes?" The policewoman took a seat on the edge of a sofa, her partner next to her. "Can you bring us up to date?"

His parents' eyes turned to Mark, and he cleared his throat before recounting what had happened. Always the facts when the police were involved. Not guesses or what-ifs: they never helped.

When he finished, the policeman looked up from his notebook. "So, your sister claims she can see fairies?"

Mum leaned forward, her gaze flicking between the officers.

"Well, mostly she hears them." Dad gave a slight shrug. "She hasn't been well in the past."

In the past, that was the key. Mark had hoped never to be replaying this scene again.

The officers exchanged glances, and this time it was the woman who spoke. "And this illness is of a mental nature?"

"Yes," said Dad. The look Mum shot him could have set off a new Ice Age. "She's had three acute episodes."

"She's *not* sick." Mum sat so far forward she was nearly off her seat, and it started to make sense why she hadn't wanted the police. Amy had been well for so long. Life had been mostly normal for years; it had been easy to relegate her episodes to a long-buried past. To be back in this state of worry about where she was and what she was doing was hard to accept. Better to pretend Amy had gone for a walk and would return soon, albeit with some mad, lurid tale about fairies, than face the alternative.

The policewoman raised her eyebrows. "You're telling me she really does see fairies?"

"*Hear*," said Dad and Mark nodded. It was important to make the distinction: the doctors said hearing voices was not uncommon. Making them a physical reality was a step further than any of them wanted.

"Sorry, Dad," said Mark. He drew in a deep breath, preparing for the storm from his mother. "She said she saw something yesterday."

The policeman glanced at Mark with eyes full of sympathy, as if acknowledging he was surrounded by mad people. He didn't know Mark was just as crazy with worry as his parents, no matter how well he hid it behind a veneer of practicality.

"What did she see yesterday?" the policeman asked.

"Fairies." He spread his hands, as if all of this was simple. "Or, at least, that's what she said they were."

"Which ones?" asked mum, leaning forwards. "Did she tell you what was there?"

He ignored her and faced the police officers. "My mother believes Amy is in contact with the fairies." No doctor, or period of peace, had shaken her belief that Amy was fey, the special child touched by the fairies. He pushed away the familiar bitterness that stabbed his chest. There'd be time to deal with that later. "Dad believes they're nothing more than intrusive thoughts. She also has visual disturbances from time to time, too. Aura migraines."

It was astounding, even to himself, how matter of fact he could be, summing up what had disintegrated his parents' marriage. Well, that and the drink.

The policewoman's eyes narrowed. "Which do you believe?"

Oh, hell. Things were bad enough without forcing him to take sides. On the other hand, the police had to judge the risk to Amy one way or another. He glanced at his mother who sat, hands clenched on her lap, waiting, he was sure, for the blow.

"I believe the doctors, the same as Dad does." To believe the alternative wasn't just ridiculous, but hopeless. Madness could be cured. He'd never heard anyone offer an opinion on curing the other. He shrugged. "Does it matter? She's missing and needs to be found."

"I have to ask," said the policewoman. "Is Amy dangerous to others?"

"No!" Mum was first, but Mark and his dad were close behind.

"Good." The policeman closed his notebook as if that decided things. "And the other lad on the hill? He's looking for her?"

"Yeah, he's been gone about an hour." A quick glance at the time made him start. "Closer to two, now."

The officer pulled at his collar and shifted in his seat. Mark tried to guess how old he was – mid-twenties, maybe, and probably not used to these sorts of interviews. He likely spent half his time dealing with sheep theft and lost tourists, not mad women looking for fairies.

"The weather on the ridge is nasty. He might have taken shelter." The policewoman squared her shoulders, and faced his parents. "We also have to ask if Amy is a danger to herself."

The question hung for a moment. Mum shook her head and mouthed no. Dad clasped his hands tighter, his eyes flitting to the sideboard. At any moment, Mark half-expected him to grab the whiskey decanter and slug the contents, no matter how old. Time stretched on, until Dad looked back at the policeman and said, slowly, "She might be."

Mum stood, her eyes hot with anger. "*You* say that! She isn't."

He faced her. "You weren't the one who found her half out of her bedroom window trying to follow the fairies." She flinched, but he went on. "The path was fifteen feet down. If I'd have been a second slower she'd have fallen." His eyes met Mark's, the unspoken history of the day when Amy had almost drowned herself in Strangford Lough, between them.

He looked miserable as he turned back to the police officers. "Yes, officers." His words were slow and sure. "I'm afraid she might well be a danger to herself."

The policeman stood. His partner said something to Mum, to comfort her judging by the low tone and the pat on her shoulder that she flinched from.

"If you could stay where we can find you, that would be helpful," said the policeman. "We'll keep you informed."

The officers left. The door closed and the silence resumed for a few long moments.

His mother finally got to her feet. "How could you?" she asked Dad. Her eyes were flinty blue, lacking warmth. "If they send her back to hospital, it'll be your fault."

"They might not," said Mark. "This might only be a brief episode. And we can't leave her out there on her own."

"He's right," said Dad. "It's going to piss down again. What if she's fallen? Do you want her lying somewhere with no one even looking for her? They only have a few hours to search before what little light there is falls."

"You *know* where she is." Mum's lips pulled back,

revealing teeth. She looked like a mother wolf, protecting her young. She pointed out the window, to the glen beyond. "She hasn't fallen. And no amount of searching will find the underworld."

Dad gave a harsh sound, somewhere between a laugh and a curse. "With the fairies, you mean? Emma, do you know how nuts that makes you sound? You must know that Amy's confused. She's sick. Surely you can see that?"

She sank into her seat and bowed her head. Mark moved to the arm of her chair and rubbed his mother's shoulders, trying to work out the hard knots of tension. His dad stared out of the window, tracking the glenscape half-lost under the storm clouds. The silence stretched on. Whatever happened today, a new fracture had further divided his family, driven by Amy and her dreams of fairyland. One as hard to heal as all the others.

CHAPTER TWELVE

AMY STRAIGHTENED AND scanned the bare landscape. She had no idea where she was – her only objective had been to get away and find a path back down the hill. She pressed her hand to her side, easing a stitch. At least the voices had stopped, taking the shadow-fairy with them.

All she needed to do was pick out the road and head down to it. She shaded her eyes, but couldn't find it. Nothing looked familiar: she could see no sign of the standing stones, or the B&B, just fields stretching either side of her, one leading to another.

Her leg ached. She crouched and tracked the cut on her leg, hissing at sharp pain. When she brought her hand to her face, thick blood ran down her fingers. The cut was deeper than a fence would leave, with jagged edges. The farmers often used barbed wire – that would explain it. If so, the wire would have been exposed to the elements, rusted and dirty. Not good, not at all.

She got to her feet. Mud oozed over the top of her sandals and between her toes, like the tongue of something unspeakable. It reminded her of the shadow. Long moments passed as she tried to calm herself.

Finally, she set off down the hill. As long as she descended, sooner or later, she'd reach one of the roads that carved between the glens.

A low rumble of thunder started in the distance, rolling to a crescendo that she could almost feel. She sped up, limping and slipping, mud splashing her legs. Lightning forked the sky over the hill ahead.

The storm hit, more ferocious than ever. Her dress was stuck to her in moments. Water dripped from her already-soaked hair to run in a steady stream down her face.

She quickly gave up hope of finding the road and scanned the hillside, seeking shelter. She made out a dark shape in the next field, promisingly box-like – and the only thing in sight. She pushed through the hedgerow, yelping as a thorn scratched her face. It was worth it, though: when she reached the small, ramshackle shed it had a roof and looked fairly watertight.

She pulled the door, having to give a few good tugs before it opened. The rain ran down the back of her knuckles, dripped down her legs and onto her feet. She couldn't get any wetter. With relief, she ducked into the shed.

It stank, turning her stomach. Mould and dirt; old, damp wood. Something fishy, too. A fork of lightning lit up the interior, showing all the cluttered corners, and she saw that the smell came from an open bag of animal feed.

She didn't fancy being holed up in the dark, but if she could find something to prop the door open she'd be able to see out and still be dry. She took in the array of farm tools hanging neatly from hooks along each side of the shed, and the sisal bags stored under long benches. Her gaze fell on a bag of logs propped against the back wall. They'd be heavy enough, she reckoned. She took a careful step in and reached for the bag, keeping her foot on the door.

The wind whistled and the door shot forward, scraping the length of her instep, and pushed her into the shed. It closed with a bang that drowned out her yell of pain.

Darkness slammed around her. *Oh, sweet Jesus.* She fumbled for the door, and fell against it. It didn't move. She couldn't find any latch, and when she shouldered it, the door didn't give.

A whisper came in the dark. She backed away, hands out. Another whisper. She turned her head trying to work out where it was coming from, but it was shifting around, making it impossible for her to tell. The bag of animal-feed tripped her, just behind her knees. She toppled backwards and landed against the wall of the shed, half-stunned.

Voices came, circling in the darkness, ebbing and growing with the wind. Panic seized her. She turned and started to bang on the back wall, not caring what creature ran, squirming and fast, under her hands. Her fists started to ache, but she banged harder and louder.

No one came. Whatever daylight left had been stolen by the storm, leaving only shadows around her. Rain bounced off the corrugated iron roof, some of it leaking through the joins to stream down the wall. She yelled, making herself hoarse.

Her breath hitched. She stopped hammering and sank to her haunches. The door rattled, and the roof banged, catching in the wind. The shed was more like a drum than shelter. Something skittered over her foot. She bit back a yell: if it was a spider, it was in the wrong hemisphere, it was so big.

She couldn't gather her thoughts through the noise. They started to get away from her, sending what-ifs crashing into fear. What if the skittering wasn't a spider, but something worse? Something with grasping, hooked fingers, perhaps one of the twisted brownies who'd crossed through the portal earlier? What if she was left in this shed forever? Would hunger and thirst take her before fear?

The door flew open, framing a man between shed and sky; hair slightly too long, broad shouldered like a rugby player. Simon. She stumbled to her feet and flung herself at him, beyond any embarrassment. He put his arms around her and Amy felt safer just being held by him, wet and cold though he was. They stood like that for a moment, neither speaking, and he tightened his embrace.

Leave him. That's what the Queen at Oisin's grave had said, her voice low and dangerous. Amy drew away from Simon but this time there was nowhere to go. A new fear came, sharper than any of the others. What if she had brought him into danger?

"HOW DID YOU find me?" She sat against the feed sack, Simon beside her, his body giving some warmth against the wind that came in through the open door. Lightning flashed over the hills, and clouds raced across the sky. But for the cold air, she could have been watching a movie.

"I was lucky. I got turned around on the hill and heard your shouts – the mist carried them, I think."

She frowned. "There was no mist."

"There was plenty where I was." He gave a half-laugh.

"Bloody mountains, they change every five minutes." There was a pause, and then he asked, his voice lower, "Why did you run? At the standing stones?"

The memory of the hatred carried by the voices came back to her. She couldn't tell him about the hissed threats towards him, and how she had believed them. Without hearing the voices, it would never make sense.

"Do I frighten you?" He drew away from her.

"No!" How could he think that? He made her feel safe, not scared. "It was nothing to do with that."

The slightest movement, a relaxing in his muscles, brought him back alongside her. "Then what?" he insisted. He might be kind, but his questioning was remorseless.

She drew her knees up to her chest, hugging them, and gave a slight shrug. Better to get it over with. "The voices – they tell me things that aren't true."

"The voices or the fairies?" He was surprisingly matter-of-fact. "Or are they the same thing? I'm confused."

Who wasn't? It was a relief to be asked, though – so many people who knew her didn't know how to broach the subject. And as for men – it normally took only one of her weirder moments for them to realise that kooky wasn't as cute as it sounded.

"They're the same thing," she said. How to explain it? An army of doctors had been struggling to define her for a decade. "Maybe. It's either a fantasy of mine, that the fairies are real, or, if they're not, the thoughts might just be that – thoughts. No one knows for sure." Not even her. What sort of person couldn't even tell her own mind?

"Like a psychosis?" She strained to hear an edge to his voice, the first sign of the drawing away that had happened so many times in the past, but there was nothing except muted interest.

"Maybe. The line is pretty blurred. So far no one wants to commit." She shrugged. "Except Mum. She believes the voices are the fairies. She always has."

She wanted to hit out at something. Once the doctors heard about this weekend, she could be labelled as psychotic, a label she'd have to carry throughout her life. It would be on every doctor's note. If she had a baby, they'd bring it up and question if she should be a mum. If she needed medication it would have to be balanced against whatever she'd already be on. She'd never be free of what happened this weekend.

And if she wasn't ill? If her mother was right? She didn't know which she was more frightened of: madness or the fairies, with their twisted faces and hidden intentions. She tried to keep her voice steady. "I just want them to go away."

"I can understand that." He shifted. The sacks on either side of the shed had crushed him against her. His hand fell against her arm. "Jesus, you're freezing." He shrugged his jacket off and draped it around her. "Here, it's not quite dry, but it's better than nothing."

She buried her nose into it, glad of the warmth. Faded cologne and half-dried rain replaced the fish-smell.

"There. Get warmed up." He rubbed her bare shoulder, his hand marginally warmer than her skin, brisk and businesslike. "That dress is useless in this sort of weather."

As the cold left her, so did some of the day's shock. It didn't feel so awful, to be lost on the hill. It felt like, if they had to stay until morning, she could cope. He stopped rubbing and she ducked under his arm, letting it fall against her shoulder. She sat against him, aware he was only in his thin dress shirt from the wedding. Somehow, it felt oddly intimate to watch the storm framed in the doorway.

"So," he said, "which do *you* think? Forget what the doctors say for now. Or your mother."

His voice twisted with something she couldn't quite read. Dislike? But he didn't even know her mother. Either way, it was a rarity for someone to ask what she believed instead of telling her what they did. A rarity she didn't have an answer for.

"It's hard to know." If she'd been asked a day ago, she'd have said they were thoughts which she'd learned to ignore. Thoughts that came in voices, or sometimes brought a shadow – even a shape – to the corner of her eye, but only because she was so wound up and anxious about them. The shapes had been so bleary she'd been able to blame the migraines for years, knowing that she was lying to herself just as much as the doctors.

"It must be." How could he think he was scary? He was the most patient man in the world. He squared his shoulders – trying to get comfy in the cramped space, she supposed. "Well, then, which came first – the voices or the fairies?"

That was another good question. A great one, in fact. And easy to answer. "The fairies."

There had been no voices before the little glen. She screwed her eyes up, thinking. Her memories of the glen – her real memories, not those in her dreams – were hazy, buried under long discussions with her mother: talks that had so many layers that the truth had been lost. Sometimes it felt like her memories – all of her – had been twisted over the years, and even more in the last few months. Even Mark didn't know how Mum's drillings about the fairies had grown since he'd moved out, or how tiring it had been. Reliving it in the new house, buried in a wooded lane close to the sea and the fairies the tides carried, had turned her life into a confused mix of the real and the lost. It was no wonder she'd succumbed at the wedding; she'd been due a relapse for weeks. She sat a little straighter.

"What is it?" he asked.

The shed felt like it was shrinking, becoming claustrophobic. "My mum...." She paused, trying to snatch what had flashed through her mind, but it was gone. "She's fascinated by the fairies."

"Fascinated? How?"

"She likes to know what happens and when. She talks about what I've seen and heard, and goes over it and over it."

"That sounds –" She could tell he was groping for the word, perhaps not wanting to offend her. "–odd. Shouldn't she try to give you a break? Distract you from the thoughts?"

Give me a normal life? The anger she held, always deep inside, bubbled to the surface. She'd had this argument with her mother so many times, and the answer had always been the same – that burying the fairies didn't help, that only by facing them could Amy come back to what she'd once been. Clean and untouched.

"She's trying to help," she said, loyalty winning over her anger. "She doesn't mean anything by it."

"Doesn't sound like it."

Her hands clenched around his coat, drawing it right up to her chin. He knew nothing about what it had taken to support her over the years. Once it had become clear the voices weren't going away without a fight her family had taken her to specialist after specialist. Her father had left in the end, no longer able to take the strain. Since then, it had been her mother who'd listened to Amy's nightmares, who'd supported her through episode after episode. If she had come to a conclusion that the doctors weren't helping, who could say she was wrong?

"You don't understand," she said.

"Maybe I don't." His voice softened. "And it's none of my business. Sorry if I stuck my foot in where it's not needed. But, you know – it sounds hellish."

It *was* hellish. All of it. And useless to keep rehashing.

"Should we try to get back to the house?" she asked. She couldn't tell him of the rising need in her to get away. Storm or no storm, she wanted to be on the move. Staying where the fairies could find her was dangerous – she had to get out of the glens before they could come back for her. She knew from the past that they would keep coming at her, wearing her down.

"We're dry here," he said. "I'm sure Mark will have someone searching for us. On balance – I think better here than getting tipped on."

"What do we do if they don't find us?" The hillside was dark now, properly dark, not just overcast. The grass looked a strange grey-green. No lights indicated any houses – although if she stirred herself and went out, there might be. Even so, she'd have to find her way across the fields in the dark. Apart from the possibility of breaking her ankle in a rabbit hole, she also wouldn't be able to see what was around her. She wouldn't know if she went near the standing stones again.

His silence lasted too long. He didn't have an answer. He was from Belfast, like her, with little knowledge of what to do on a hill in the middle of a storm.

"Stay here for now," he said, in the end. "I'm not going out in that. Nor should you. We'd be dead of exposure by the morning."

"But they'll keep searching?" she said. "I mean, they know we're out here."

"I expect so." He didn't sound sure, though. "But, look, we're okay for now, aren't we? We won't starve in one night. And it's not like there's a water shortage. Not with this much rain." He pulled her against his chest and her panic receded. "Here; we'll keep each other warm."

They sat, watching the lightning flash and listening to the rain beating down on the roof. She drifted into a half-sleep, memories of the standing stones mixing with images from when she'd been a child, coming together for the first time. The smell was the same as in her dreams, she realised, as if she'd wakened something on the hill, something held inside her since she was five. It focused on her. Dangerous. Her eyes snapped open, and she stared into the darkness, watching.

Chapter Thirteen

M ARK LOWERED HIS fork, not able to stomach the steak and Guinness pie he'd ordered. A particularly brutal gust shook the hotel's window in its frame. His mum turned to face it. She hadn't bothered to order dinner, but had just sat, clutching Amy's bag with thin fingers. His dad stared at the bar instead of eating.

Coming out had seemed better than sitting looking at each other in the guesthouse, especially since a return visit from the police officers had confirmed the search had been called off. Darkness could be worked around, they'd said, or the storm, but the combination made the search impossible. For now, they'd alerted the farming community to keep a watch for Amy and Simon and would recommence a full search – including helicopters and extra bodies from neighbouring forces – in the morning.

Mum shifted in her seat and hunched further over the bag. Her eyes were hard to read, settling on nothing, and her body seemed to have angles that weren't natural.

"So," Dad said, his voice strained. "What do we do

now?"

Mum glared at him. "Perhaps you should get pissed and take your mind off it. That's what you usually do."

It threatened to be a long night – it was only eight o'clock, and his mum could fight for hours if she was on form.

"Mum…" warned Mark.

"No, really, it's true."

Dad stared across the table. "I'll be doing nothing of the sort."

Would he not? His dad's shakes had got worse over dinner. He must be burning with the need for a drink; he hadn't had any all afternoon and he hadn't gone more than a half-dozen waking hours without drinking in at least a year.

Shakes or no shakes, he met his wife's eyes. "The police might need to talk to us again."

"That's never stopped you before." She clutched Amy's bag even tighter. "I remember plenty of nights waiting for calls, while you got piss—"

Oh hell: someone needed to stop her before she really got going. Mark reached across the table and laid his hand on hers. It was so tightly clutched he could feel how thin her skin was, stretched over her knuckles. "Mum." His voice came out stronger than he'd expected. "You're upset. Don't say things you'll regret in the morning."

Her gaze swivelled to him and he braced for the onslaught, but she just shook her head and looked out the window. As usual, he wasn't worth fighting like Dad, or doting on like Amy. He was just Mark, who could be kicked out and discarded, reduced to a phone call in the evenings. One day it would stop hurting.

She turned her attention back to his dad. "I'll regret

nothing. You're a lush."

"I might be." For all his faults, denial had never been Dad's style. "But you're the one who encouraged Amy with all this fairy crap. If it wasn't for you, we wouldn't be here. It's all a bloody farce."

Mark rubbed his hand over his eyes. The eternal argument, round and round: the fairies were real; they couldn't be: Amy wasn't mad; she had to be. "Guys, not here, eh?"

"Stay out of this, Mark." His dad's words were cold and dismissive, leaving Mark speechless. He'd been good to his father, bailing him out of more shit than Amy or Mum knew about. He didn't deserve to be dismissed. He tried to calm down, knowing that joining the slanging match wouldn't help, but the anger was biting deep like it rarely did. Anger, and shame at being the wrong child at the table, at being Mark instead of Amy, the normal one who didn't need attention and could be dismissed.

"Right," he said, his words tight. "I'll just watch then, shall I?"

"What do you mean keeping the farce going?" said his mum. She hadn't even looked at him. "Which farce? The one where we pretend the doctors have ever made a difference? At least I'm trying to help Amy. When did you last try?"

"Enough." Dad ran his hands through his hair, but his eyes flicked up through his unkempt fringe, towards the bar. He looked as desperate as a man could be. He wouldn't last much longer, and then he'd get pissed and the whole evening would turn into a snarl of guilt and recriminations. "She knows she can come up to the boat any time she wants."

"A boat you've barely room to stand up in. Good for you."

Mark stood. He'd spent half his childhood trying to referee fights, he knew when the point of no return had been reached. He grabbed his borrowed cagoule from the back of the spare seat where it had gently steamed during dinner. "If the two of you want to fight, go ahead. You don't need me for an audience."

Neither of his parents tried to stop him, even though he paused long enough for them to try. He strode to the door and roughly shoved it open. Rain hit his face, laced with salt from the sea. Across the road, in the harbour, masts chimed a song directed by the gale. Amy was out in this, and their parents wanted to trade insults.

He held his cagoule in one hand and let the rain stream through his hair and down his neck. If he thought he'd get away with it, he'd strip to his boxers and stand, shivering, so that when – *if* said a small voice, hastily dismissed – Amy came back, he'd be able to say that he understood what she'd gone through. The cold and wet part at least. Her confusion and fear, her desperate wish for all the fairy crap to stop happening and normality take its place; that, he couldn't experience, no matter how hard he'd tried. But she'd never experienced being him – waiting, not knowing if she was all right. She'd never known the sheer helplessness of watching her.

He walked to the pub on the corner of the main street, past a narrow street housing the entrance to the pub's delivery yard. The pub's signage was dirty and missing letters, the windows had rusted bars. The side door's shutter had been daubed with graffiti declaring someone in this village was gay. He bet they didn't drink here, then.

Which meant the pub was perfect for him. Two doormen, huddled in the porch for shelter, looked him up and down, taking in his soaked hair and day-old wedding clothes. One glanced at the cagoule, carried instead of worn, but didn't comment. Instead, he pushed the door open and let Mark duck inside.

Mark shouldered his way through a crowd which had gathered just inside the door, and approached the bar. A second, rowdier group were at the far end, watching a big screen showing the footie. Man U at home to Liverpool; he'd forgotten it was on tonight. They'd been talking about it all week at work – he even had a sweep for it – but work was too distant to matter, beyond the wedding where he'd taken his eye off the ball and fucked up.

Guilt burned in him and he welcomed it. He deserved to feel guilty. He'd known Amy had gone wandering after the speeches; he'd watched her pass the back windows of the function room and stop to talk with Simon on the bridge. He'd thought about going to get her but he'd been chatting at the bar and it was during the lull when people liked to clear their head before the disco. Besides, Mum had noticed her, too – he knew that, because she'd stopped at the window and watched Amy. It had been easy to tell himself if Mum wasn't bothered, he shouldn't be.

All excuses. If he'd gone after Amy, she mightn't have got it into her head that going to the waterfall was a good idea. If he'd known that was what she'd fixated on, he'd have agreed to go back to Belfast and not stay for the disco. Nothing would have happened. His fault, again, for not being quick enough to stop her, for not being able to find her, for being the one who was all right and safe, even though he was the big brother, the protector.

A roar went up from the footie crowd, and a complaint about the ref. The language and range of tattoos confirmed he'd found the sort of bar he'd been looking for.

"What can I get you?" The barman leaned towards Mark, his voice raised over the noise.

Mark paused. If it were his dad he'd order a triple just to start the evening off, provided someone else was paying. Mark took his wallet out of his pocket, and reminded himself he wasn't his dad.

"Double Jack Daniels," he said. "Straight."

The barman nodded and turned to the optics. Mark took the chance to look around the rest of the bar, picking out different people and groups until....

There, standing by the alcove of what looked to be a second lounge, a tall blonde girl threw her head back in a laugh. A bloke leaned one arm on the wall by her head, so that she was caught between the wall and him. The man was laughing, but there was tension in his shoulders, a possessiveness impossible to fake. Mark eyed her up and down, taking everything in – and there was plenty to take in – and then checked out her companion: he was as tall as Simon and almost as broad. He stayed just a little too close to the girl and when she shifted to get more space, he moved and took back his dominance. He was perfect.

"Here's your drink."

Mark handed the barman twenty quid. He lifted the glass and knocked it back, welcoming the burn as the whiskey went down, not smooth like Irish malt, but harsh, almost vicious. He banged the glass onto the bar. "Another, cheers."

The barman hesitated, obviously trying to work out if Mark was drunk, but Mark met his gaze square on. Not yet, he wasn't. The barman nodded, satisfied, and went back to the optic, filling a new glass. This time, Mark took it away from the bar, cradling it as he went through to the second lounge. He passed the couple by the alcove and her perfume hit him: floral and high, far from the sense of heavy air that had chased him all day.

He took up position, leaning on the wall opposite the couple, and watched them through the ebb and flow of people, never moving his attention from the girl. He should time this. In Belfast, it could take an hour, but here where everyone knew each other and a stranger stood out… soon. Slowly, he drank and stared. The woman met his eyes a couple of times, and then started to deliberately focus on the bloke instead. Even so, her attention kept coming back to Mark, under her lashes, quick glances and then away. He wondered if she'd try to flirt with him, or scare him off. It was always hard to be sure.

She tugged her boyfriend's sleeve and whispered something to him. Scare him off then. Good; it saved time. Mark took a deep breath, savouring the moment when the boyfriend turned and looked at him. The man raised his chin, and Mark raised his glass in return. He took a last swig of the bourbon, welcoming the burning as a precursor to something deeper, more meaningful. Not penance, exactly, that seemed too holy. Absolution? Perhaps.

The boyfriend shouldered his way through the crowd. He stopped at a table and spoke to two blokes sitting there. They looked up at Mark with sharp interest, and got to their feet. Both were tall and ruddy faced. Probably farmers. One stopped to drain his drink, watching Mark as he did.

Excitement, mingling with low fear, fought the whiskey in Mark's stomach. The boyfriend stopped in front of him, his lips drawn back from bared teeth. His two companions took up a flanking position, giving Mark nowhere to escape to.

He took a deep breath. *Let the show begin.*

INTERLUDE I

*A*MY ALWAYS ATTRACTED *comments about her looks. People said she was like a fairy when she was young. As she grew older, the comments changed to otherworldly and ethereal. Fae, I used. Some mentioned her dark eyes, like deep pools and impossible to read. No matter how quietly I watched her, careful not to be noticed, she'd catch me and look at me with those eyes and smile, an old smile that tormented me. A smile that had walked this earth before.*

Amy was nine, the night I learned for sure. Mark was away overnight, at his first scout camp, and Phil was working on his damned boat, his hiding place from me even then.

I'd planned the night for months. We'd go early to the park, have a picnic before it got dark, and stay for the open-air theatre show. It was going to be a mother/daughter night out and if Phil hadn't mentioned the boat in front of Amy it would have been perfect. Instead, she complained about putting on a dress in place of her sailing duds, and then about the picnic and the sandwiches I'd cut into stars. She wanted to eat on deck and have sausages from Phil's little stove instead. She whined and whined, until I was ready to call the whole thing off.

But, no. Mark was getting his treat; she needed hers. We got to the park as darkness was falling. Lights hung in all the trees. Pixies, carrying light sticks and lanterns, came from the depths of the park and sprinkled the kids, and half the adults, with fairy dust. They told us to make a wish and I made mine: the same one as always.

The sandwiches were Amy's favourite ham, and we had crisps and little cubes of cheese and melon. We ate and drank pink lemonade while we chatted, everyday things about school, and friends, and plans. That's how cunning she was; she could have passed with anyone.

The golden lights on the first stage came up, the focal point of the park. We watched, entranced, until Snow White bit the apple and the stage went dark. Amy drew in a gasp, and I turned to her. "Good?"

She nodded, but looked worried. "Why did she take the apple? It was from a stranger."

I paused to consider the tough question. Amy was in the stranger-danger years, and I daren't erode what the school taught. But Amy needed to know that strangers don't always have evil faces. Sometimes they're pretty. Sometimes you already know them. "Maybe no one told her to be careful," I said, and Amy accepted it.

The next stage lit up behind us, and we had to turn to watch. Snow White lay encased in her glass coffin, her cheeks rose-red, and she was so pretty Amy gave a little gasp. This stage was white and cold. Dark trees loomed on the backdrop, their branches reaching like fingers.

The dwarves – vertically challenged miners, according to the cast list, funny little men to the kids – hi-ho'ed their way in and did some acrobatics. I'm not sure the youngest dwarf landing in the crowd was intentional, but it made Amy laugh.

He clambered back on stage and the seven of them hoisted the coffin on their shoulders, and took Snow White away. The stage snapped into darkness. The park was silent; the hundreds of children and parents were as still as glass.

I smoothed Amy's hair. I wanted to take her on my knee and hold her close enough that she couldn't escape, but Amy hated being held like that. Instead, I watched the tree-lights dancing in her eyes.

The third stage came up to the right. Pastel pink, shifting through to green. The crowd gave soft ooohs. A prince cantered through the park on his hobby horse and arrived on the stage. He bent and kissed Snow White, who stretched, drawing the moment out, and sat up. She asked children for their wishes. Amy closed her eyes and mouthed hers. I tried to read her lips, but couldn't, and she'd never tell. I knew that. Amy was good at keeping secrets.

The lights went out. I started to pick up our picnic plates. Amy ran to play with some friends from school.

When I looked for her, seconds later, she was gone. My heart thundered. I spun in a circle until I was dizzy. Railway tracks ran along the embankment above the park. One of the infrequent trains roared past. What if the fence was broken? Visions of Amy caught under the train, her arms thrashed out and dead, filled me. Hot fear attacked from all sides. I dropped the picnic basket, ready to run to the tracks when something on the middle stage – the white, cold one – took my attention.

It was Amy, pushing tendrils of fake forest aside. She spun in her flared dress, round and round, captured in fairyland. The white light cast her face half into shadow, making her look thinner and older.

I sank to the ground and watched, and knew I was seeing her secret. I saw her smile at something I couldn't see, dance to a tune I couldn't hear, and drank in my fairy daughter.

Chapter Fourteen

T HEY LED HIM round the back of the pub; it was always round the back or down an alley. Mark allowed himself to be marched past the bouncers, who seemed inexplicably interested in something across the road, and up the side street. The two big guys jostled against him, giving him no room to run; the boyfriend led the way. Fear sank into his stomach, leaden, mixed with self-loathing. God, he wasn't right in the head.

The guy on his left shoved into the back yard of the pub and he stumbled against a shuttered doorway; the delivery entrance, presumably. The two goons fell back. A single spotlight angled at the doorway half-blinded him, so all he could see were the blokes' shadows.

"You want to learn to keep your eyes to yourself." One of the shadows, the biggest, broke from the others, approaching slowly.

Mark licked his lips. There was still time to get out of this. A quick *sorry, I was drunk*, a promise to piss off and never be seen again, and he might be allowed away. If he could beat himself up, he would. It'd be easier.

Easier, maybe, but it wouldn't touch the hurt in him; he knew, he'd tried. He laughed, and it was harsh. He lifted his chin, defiant, not shaking at all. That would come later. "But she had such good tits."

"That's it." The big lad appeared out of the light, flanked by his two mates. "Hold him."

Hands closed around his biceps, encircling and tight; shoved him roughly against the shutter. Fear jumped in him, the sick knowledge that he'd gone too far and a kicking was coming. Please, God, let it do what he needed. Last time, he'd crawled home and had still been filled with self-hatred the next morning. After years of family counselling, he knew why he did it, and what hurt he was trying to hide from. Understanding, though, was neither a consolation nor a reason to stop.

"Bring it on, then," he said.

The bloke's fist caught him square on the jaw. His head crashed against the shutter. They weren't worried about anyone from the pub coming out, evidently. He grunted when a second punch took him in the stomach, so hard he'd have doubled over but for the hands holding him upright.

"More?" asked the big lad. He cracked his knuckles. "Make sure you learn to keep your eyes to yourself?"

"Try it, you culchie bastard." His voice was slurred, his jaw thick and slow. More. Always more.

The bloke's hand pulled back, a ring glinting in the light. Mark held his breath, waiting, waiting, and then it hit, under his right eye. A burst of pain. His eye started to close. His head thudded off the shutter and he yelled at a sharp line of agony. He'd be lucky if he didn't need stitches for that one. He gasped a breath, but the adrenalin was flowing now.

"Fuck you," he slurred. He tried to grin, but was sure it must be lopsided. He could barely feel one side of his mouth. "And your girl."

Another punch, this time in the ribs. This was it; what he needed. One of the goons pulled his head back, and he let them, ready for the next blow. He deserved this.

"Hey!" someone yelled. "Stop it!" A new shadow appeared from further back. Mark squinted at it. The voice hadn't been the soft local brogue, but harsher, from Belfast. *Oh shit.*

The fighter turned to face the newcomer, his hands bunched, his breathing heavy. "Fuck off, Granda."

"Leave him alone." Dad appeared from under the light, his beard and hair matted in the rain like a wild-man's. He pointed at Mark. "He's with me."

The big man looked at Mark with a smile that showed his teeth. "Come back in half an hour. You can pick up what's left from the pavement."

Dad reached for the bloke. With his good eye, Mark could see the muscles corded along his arm, strong from working the ropes on the boat. He grabbed the lad's shoulder and tightened his grip, spinning him around. "Let him go."

The man knocked his hand away. "Do you want some of the same?" He brought his fists up. "He came on to my girl. Scared her, the way he was watching her."

Dad faced the big lad, square on. He had no chance; the guy had three inches on him as well as several pounds. And twenty years.

"Dad…" said Mark. This was *his* fight. If his dad got a kicking, how was that going to help? "Just go."

"Nope." Dad stepped back, but he stayed tense and

alert. He wasn't leaving, that was obvious, but he put his hands up as if in surrender. His dad had a good history of overstepping the mark when drunk, too – he knew how to placate. "I'm not here for any trouble. He's sorry." He glared at Mark. "Aren't you?"

Reality crashed back, carried by the look in his father's eyes. He'd have to explain this to him. And to Mum; he'd be black and blue in the morning. His face throbbed and his stomach cramped and ached. He looked down and saw blood, big drops that merged with the rain. What the hell had he been thinking? "Yeah. I'm sorry."

"Look at him," said Dad. "He's not worth it."

"Fuck off," said the big man. "Or you'll join him." But his voice lacked conviction; the interruption had stolen his momentum.

Dad jerked his head towards the street. "Let him go, or I'll tell the bar staff what's going on."

"You won't have any teeth left to talk through." The lad advanced but Dad skittered back, keeping out of range. He might be older and out-muscled, but he was fast.

"Shay!" The lad holding Mark's right arm loosened his hold. "If Fergie gets a complaint about this, you'll get barred. He said that last time."

"Fuck Fergie. There're other pubs."

"None that'll let you in."

The big lad's nostrils flared but he lowered his fists. "Stay there, Grandad." He approached Mark, who tensed, ready for another punch, but the bloke reached out and grasped his chin, hard, sending pain shooting through his jaw as he tilted it up. Mark stared at him, gulping for breath.

"If I see you near Jen again, I'll take you apart." The lad's eyes were hard, unflinching. "Right?"

God, yes; all right. Mark licked the rain from his lips, tainted with the iron taste of blood. "Right." He wanted to tell him to say sorry to Jen, that he hadn't meant to scare her.

"Let him go."

The blokes holding Mark dropped him. He doubled to his knees with a low groan. He hurt all over.

"Make sure he's gone in the next few minutes, Grandad."

Feet crunched over broken glass. Mark looked up through his wet hair. They left the yard. Silence fell. He pushed himself to his feet, but didn't say anything. He wiped his mouth with the back of his hand and looked at the blood: a lot more of it than he'd anticipated.

"What the hell were you thinking?" asked Dad, finally. "What use is it if you land yourself in hospital?"

"I made a mistake. I eyed up the wrong girl." If Dad had been drinking he might even buy the excuse. "It could happen to anyone."

The rain beat down, hissing as it hit the light. Dad shook his head; even drunk he wasn't an idiot, and his eyes were still, miraculously, clear. Mark must have got him on the way into the pub.

"You didn't make a mistake," said his dad. He lifted Mark's chin, gentler than Shay had been. Mark winced but didn't pull away, and his dad took his time, taking in his mostly-closed eye, his split lip. "You were bloody lucky I decided a walk was preferable to fighting with your mother."

"A trip to the bar, you mean." Mark couldn't resist saying it; his father had no business coming off with the holier-than-thou-shite. Not after the number of times Mark had bailed him out. "Don't let me stop you."

"On my way back, actually," said his Da. "I spent a quarter of an hour looking at the optics in the bar up the road before I walked out." His face twisted. "It's a better one than this dive; you obviously knew what you were looking for."

It made no sense, but his dad was definitely sober; he didn't smell of drink nor slur any of his words.

"You walked out?" Mark asked. His dad hadn't walked out of a bar before kicking out time in years.

"Aye." Dad didn't quite meet his eyes. "I thought, maybe…" He swallowed and he looked older than he was, like he *was* Mark's grandad. "Hell, I thought when we found Amy I should be sober for her." He gave an ironic smile. "I didn't expect it to be you who needed me."

"I'm sure you didn't." Mark rubbed his jaw and winced. "It's good you were here." He started to walk towards the street, hand over his stomach, feeling ancient.

"What are you going to say to your mother?"

Mark gave a harsh laugh. "Dad, I could turn up in a body bag and be lucky if she'd notice."

"Is that it?" His dad stopped. "You thought you were due some attention when your sister's missing in the middle of a storm?"

Put that way, it sounded awful. And it wasn't even close to the truth. "No." Any words he might have had died on his lips – he'd never be able to explain what it was like to always be the one who was okay, who was safe, who didn't have fairies driving him insane, and *not* sound like a selfish bastard. "It's about…." How to admit that this kept him sane, and when he was sane he could hold things together? That holding things together for Amy was all he could to offer her?

"What then?"

"Do you see me as the centre of anyone's attention?"

"No, but –"

He nodded. "I can't keep Amy safe and I can't keep you sober." Dad winced, but Mark had to go on; he couldn't stop. "I can't deal with Mum when she's the way she is tonight." His voice broke, but he forced the admission: "If I'm hurting, I'm not thinking."

"Oh, shit, that's…."

Fucked up, at best. Not that it should be a surprise, given the rest of the family.

His dad's face softened. "Your mum was planning to go back to the guesthouse. Let's dig up a taxi and go too. Slip in without her seeing. If you put some ice on that face, you mightn't look too bad by the morning." He met Mark's eyes. "And in the meantime, you and I are going to have a talk about things."

Must we? Mark followed his dad from the alley, hand trailing against the wall for support. He supposed they must. It was probably past due that someone forced him to it.

CHAPTER FIFTEEN

A MY WOKE TO find the shed in darkness. The storm had eased, leaving only popping noises as the rain dripped from the corrugated roof. Simon must have closed the door at some point and, if not for the biting cold and prehistoric spiders, the shed might have been cosy.

He had curled awkwardly between a bench and her, his head dropped to his chest, clearly asleep. Carefully, she shifted away and sat, staring into the darkness, trying to work out what had wakened her.

Shadows surrounded her, long shadows that had no beginning or end. She strained her ears, senses alert, and became aware of a familiar smell, almost lost in the fishiness of the animal feed. Her hands clenched in front of her, as if they could keep her safe. It was the smell from the pathway earlier, a stench that made her think of graves opened in the rain and left to grow old and rotted. She unclenched her hands and put her arms around each other, hugging herself.

A pair of eyes opened in the darkness, a few feet away. She bit back a yell. It was her imagination, nothing more.

She blinked, hard, but when she looked again the eyes were still there, glinting white against the darkness. Rows of them, more than she wanted to count. She braced herself, knowing what had to come next.

Amy. Her name was sweetly seductive. Simon stirred, but his breathing soon went back to normal. She wished he'd woken and disturbed the fairies. Her hand went to her throat, feeling for her acorn, but it wasn't there. The ribbon had broken, she remembered, and she'd been holding it when she'd went to sleep. She must have dropped it.

Sharp fear took hold. With her acorn, the fairies couldn't touch her. They could talk to her, and haunt her, but they couldn't take her. Without it… *Kill him.* The voice brought a stabbing fear, below her ribs. The sharp surety of it took her breath away. She shook her head, no, but the words burrowed into her, breaking through her resolve. She looked past the eyes, taking in the walls hung with tools. Sharp tools, she remembered. Deadly. Her right hand itched. She glanced at the sleeping Simon. It could be done in moments. He'd hardly feel it.

Now. So you can come to us. The eyes crept forwards. There were more of them. Images of long ago, of a green glen, of welcoming hands taking hers. If she did this, she could join them forever. She'd never have to fight again.

Temptation bit, a yearning in the depths of her stomach. She crawled across the dirty floor. She needed to get to the shelf and onto her feet to reach the tools. She tried to remember what was stored – a shovel, she was sure, and a tethering spike. Either would do the job. She crawled quicker, but her foot caught on a sack, knocking something off the shelf above. It fell to the wooden floor with a thunk.

"Amy?" Simon's voice held the confusion of someone

woken from a deep sleep. "Is that you?"

The eyes vanished, as if they'd never been there. The smell went away, too, replaced by the sick smell of fish. The need to crawl forward, the murderous urge, had vanished, and she found herself rocking back onto her heels.

"It's me," she said. Her voice sounded too thin, even to her own ears.

"Are you all right?"

She couldn't lie. Even in the darkness, he'd know. "They're here," she said.

"The fairies?" He didn't sound worried. "I can't see them."

Of course he couldn't. They'd never show themselves. "They're here, and they're dangerous. I think we should go."

"Go? It's the middle of the night. We'd end up back in Belfast quicker than we'd find the house." He didn't mention that they might not reach anywhere – that they could get turned around forever, or fall into a ditch and die of exposure – and she was glad of that. Regardless, it would be better than staying here. He didn't understand the impulse, the watching eyes, the hatred in the air.

"They don't like you," she said. They hate you. They'll kill you.

"Well, I'm not keen on them, either. I'm stuck on a mountain over the head of them." He touched her bare arm. "And you're freezing."

She didn't feel freezing; she felt too hot. He drew her back and draped his coat over her, keeping a corner for himself.

"Just sit for a while," he said. "They don't seem to come out when I'm watching."

No, they wanted her alone. She put her head on his chest and something of her old self come back. She'd like to sit like this and not worry about the voices, not believe they would return. Simon didn't talk and neither did she, as if they'd gone beyond words.

"Close your eyes." He sounded tired. "By the time you open them it'll be morning."

She didn't dare. She stayed against him but kept her eyes open, alert for the fairies. Simon's breathing steadied. She tried to think what to do. Not for herself, but for him. She shivered, the deep tremor of fever, and touched the gash on her leg. The skin around it was swollen and when she lifted her fingers away they peeled from the skin.

She turned her head, grazing Simon's shirt with her lips. Two of his buttons had parted and she could just make out his chest, the skin silvery in the darkness, rising and falling.

Her fear receded, as if he might be able to hold her in the real world. It was no wonder the fairies had moved against him – they must be able to feel the threat he presented to them. No one else made her feel so connected to them and the world around them.

She stayed for another moment, drinking in his steady breaths, the heaviness of his arm on her. He'd made her laugh last night, and this morning. Even when she'd got him stuck in this shed overnight, he'd been good-humoured about it. She raised her head and kissed him, gently, on the lips, drawing away quickly when he murmured something.

"I'm sorry," she whispered, too quietly to be heard. She could not stay and allow the fairies to take him. She had to fight for whatever future she had. Tonight, while she still had strength. She scrabbled around for her acorn, ignoring the soft things that moved under her touch until her fingers closed around the hard metal. She could not leave Simon in this place, surrounded by them, without some kind of safety. She slipped it into his pocket.

Already the first eyes in the darkness had returned. She gave Simon a last, quick hug, wishing everything could be different. She lifted her chin. She would not go back to the stone circle. She would get down the hill and out of this place with its shadows and shifting danger. Once she did, she'd reclaim her life – her life, not the fairies' – and learn to put the voices behind her.

CHAPTER SIXTEEN

THE CAR PULLED up outside the B&B in darkness as absolute as the previous night.

"Wait a second." Dad paid the taxi man, and handed Mark the bag of frozen peas he'd picked up at a garage. "When we go in, go straight to the room. I'll put your mother off the scent."

Mark opened the side door but the house was in darkness – his mother must have already gone up to her room. He hurried down the hall, dripping water into the thick carpet. Mum's door was shut and no noise came from beyond it. Even so, as Mark passed he half expected it to open and him to be left explaining to both parents at once what had happened. Only when he reached his own room did he take a full breath. He was shivering worse in the heat than he had been outside. His hand shook as he tried the handle.

"I'll get it." It was the first time his dad had ever had the steadier hands, Mark reckoned. The door swung open.

"Get out of those wet clothes." Dad stripped his own

jumper off – without a coat the rain had soaked in, and when he dropped it on the floor it gave a soft plop. "Hurry. I don't need you getting pneumonia."

Mark pulled off his cagoule and shirt, which was so wet it peeled off him like an orange skin. His teeth were chattering, and he grabbed a towel from the nearest bed and wrapped it around him. He couldn't tell if it was from the cold or shock, but the strength left his legs. He sat on the edge of the bed, hunched forwards, feeling like a man of eighty.

"Take your time," said his dad. "You've had a hell of a night."

Shock, it seemed: the heat hadn't eased his shivering. He looked down. Along the top of his stomach muscles a yellowed bruise stood out in stark relief against his white skin. He waited for the shudders to pass, swallowing nausea, and kicked off his soaked shoes. They were ruined, and they'd been new for the wedding.

His dad vanished into the bathroom. "Anything broken?" he called.

Mark prodded his ribs, gingerly, and felt around his mouth with his tongue. Nothing seemed out of place. "I don't think so."

"That's something." Dad came back with a flannel. "Here, put the peas in that and hold it against your eye. You're a sorry sight."

"Yeah." He winced at the sharp cold on his broken skin.

"So, what happened?" Dad sniffed, like the connoisseur he was. "Whiskey, was it?"

It was amazing he hadn't named the brand. "Yeah."

"Mark, walls give blood easier than this." Dad rubbed his eyes, squeezing them shut as he did. "You'll have to talk to me sometime."

Mark's mouth opened and closed. He'd never been this freaked out. Other times he'd gone out looking for trouble, yes, but he'd always made it home to bed, usually half-comatosed, before he'd had to face what he'd done. In the morning it was easy to lie to himself; here, in this room, the dark night outside broken only by starlight, he had no hiding place.

"You can tell me, son." Dad's voice was steady and calm. "Whatever it is, I'll have done worse. You know that."

He did. Still, he looked at his feet. A barn owl screeched in the distance, and it was easy to believe what May had said about this place being different. Perhaps here, he could tell someone all that had happened.

"And however you look at it, it could be worse." His dad gave a grim smile. "It beats killing yourself with drink. How often have you done this?"

"A few times."

"Does your mum know?"

Mark gave a sour laugh. "Probably. We haven't talked about it. To be honest, we haven't talked about a lot, me and her, in the last couple of months."

"Since you moved out."

The laugh turned to a choke; his dad knew nothing about what had been going on. He'd done a sterling job of hiding. "Since I was kicked out, you mean."

Dad blinked. "She told me you had moved closer to work."

"Bullshit." He'd tried to tell his dad what had happened, but when he was sober he hadn't answered any calls, and when pissed he forgot half of what had been said. Mark turned the ice-pack around and pressed his eye with the other side. "Mum made me move out."

"When?"

"Just after Amy's eighteenth." Mark flicked his fingers, calculating the time. Jesus. Six months. What had been going on during that time to get Amy into her current state? Amy hadn't said, and his mother sure as hell wasn't sharing. "She said she'd pay for a deposit, on a rental I hadn't asked for, from the house sale."

The sale of their family home had finally gone through, after two years on the credit-crunched market. Dad had refused his share, claiming the boat was cheap to run and the profits should be used for the kids.

"I didn't mean for her to do that with the money," Dad said. "I thought it might get you a car or something. So, what happened? She asked if you wanted an apartment and you said no?"

"Yeah." Mark dabbed at his eye and looked at the towel dubiously. "I need a clean one." He made his way over to the bathroom, his movements stiff. "I wasn't happy with Amy living in the new house. The trees were so close they were knocking on her bedroom window and the beach was only a few minutes walk away. She started going down there a couple of times a day. She said she could see things in the waves, shapes, but didn't know what they were." He didn't need to be looking at his father to know how hard that would hit – they'd both been with Amy the last time she'd seen things in the tide. A memory of circling water came back, cold against his waist, rising as he'd waded forwards, the rope from his father's boat looped around him. "I was worried she was building up to an episode and didn't want to be far away."

"Did you tell your mum?"

"Not in so many words. You know what she's like. She'd have gone off on one if I'd have suggested we should do anything to stop Amy." He raised one hand and made a quote mark in the air, miming to himself. "'She's not sick, she's just special. All we can do is keep her safe'." His face twisted in the bathroom mirror and he hastily grabbed a towel and stalked back into the bedroom. His dad was easier to face than himself.

"I can see why you didn't push it." Dad looked at his hands. It was impossible to tell what he was feeling. Guilt, probably, and useless anger, too – the sort that built and curdled with nothing to take it out on.

"Anyway…." Mark sat on the room's single seat, steadier than when he'd come in. "We fought. A lot. She locked me out. Amy let me back in. Mum threw my clothes into black bags and gave them to the recycling. I bought more. She changed the locks." He gave a helpless shrug, not sure how to convey how unmovable his mother had been. "I gave in and took a flat-share, near enough for Amy to come up every day. I bought her a monthly ticket 'cos Mum tried to keep her from seeing me by taking the money from her purse."

He should have taken Amy with him the day he'd left and not told their mother where she was. Except – this mother, the one who'd change locks on him, who had forced him out, wasn't one he'd known before. She'd never been a warm mother, no, and hard to reach sometimes, but she'd always cared. He hadn't known how to handle the change in her any more than Amy had.

"Amy was furious. They fought all the time, but Mum was… nuts about it. Taking Amy's bankcards into work with her and locking the house from the outside." He shook his head. "I've never known her to do anything like it before. I thought I'd find somewhere bigger, somewhere near the art college so that Amy could move in with me. That was the hell of it – Mum was delighted when Amy got into college. But by the time I left, I didn't know what she planned to do when the term started – if she'd even let her go. It wasn't like she could be hidden away." None of it made any sense.

"And did your mum give a reason for being so – determined?" Dad sounded shocked. "It's not like her. Jesus, it was the only thing I didn't worry about; how she was looking after the pair of you."

Mark swallowed, remembering the harsh words of his final night in the house, words he'd tried to forget in his attempt to keep Mum on side and not give her any reason to turn further against him.

"She said I was a grown up and needed to stand on my own feet." He gave something that might have been a laugh. "I was doing a good job of that tonight, wasn't I?"

"Jesus, Mark, I'm sorry," Dad said. The apology sounded as weak as it was, and Mark acknowledged it with nothing more than a sharp nod. "Your mum....?" he went on. His voice carried an edge of something Mark didn't quite understand. "Did she seem ... normal? Not sick or anything?"

Sick? Mark decided he didn't want to know – anything that made his dad this wary shouldn't be touched. Not in their family.

"Not sick, no," he said. "She thinks she keeps Amy safe. But Amy's old enough to want to branch out – she's had nights out with her friends and even a few dates. I think Mum's scared."

"Scared? Your mother?"

"Yeah." He shrugged. "It's hard to explain. One minute we were singing *Happy Birthday* and making wishes, and then... she changed." His voice broke then, finally. He was amazed he'd held together this long. He gave an angry swipe at his eyes but it was coming now, the guilt; the sure knowledge it was his fault. That he'd done something by omission that had changed things, like in the little glen when he'd got caught up in fishing and hadn't even realised Amy was missing. "And I don't know what the hell I did to bring it on."

"Oh, son." Dad came over to the chair and sat on the arm, hand on his bare shoulder, and suddenly Mark was shuddering and couldn't stop crying. Even when the wind got up enough to remind him he wasn't the person in the most danger, he couldn't stop. The rational part of him, the part that had attended family counselling for years assured him it was for the best.

Why, then, did it hurt so bloody much?

CHAPTER SEVENTEEN

SIMON WOKE WITH a start, cold to the bone. A dawn sky was visible through the shed's spider-framed door, a door that was wide open. He sat up, his body cramped and protesting, and looked around the conspicuously empty shed.

"Oh, shitting hell. Not again." He jumped to his feet, fighting panic, and pulled his jacket on. His ankle protested but it took his weight, thankfully: he had more pressing things to worry about. Amy hadn't been well last night – he'd felt her head against him and had been sure she was starting a fever. He'd planned to get her out of here and down the hill first thing.

He spilled out of the shed, into the muddy field. She was nowhere to be seen. He had no idea how long she'd been away – the last thing he remembered was holding her and being aware, dimly awake, that she'd kissed him.

"Amy!" Her name echoed, mocking him. "Amy!"

His hands made fists at his side, helpless and useless. She had run from him again. God knew, if anyone could fuck things up it was him, but he couldn't think what he'd done this time. What had made him think he could help someone as obviously disturbed as Amy? Why had he even thought she'd *want* him to?

He scrambled down the hill, ignoring his ankle's complaint at the steep descent. The ground evened out and he thrust his hands into his jacket pockets as protection against the cold morning air. His knuckle brushed against something cool and hard in the right pocket. He fished out the little acorn Amy had worn.

A lump came into his throat. She'd said the necklace kept her safe from the fairies. His hand clutched over it. "Ah, hell, Amy." He looked up to the sky, watching the streak of light spread, and barely trusted himself to think what the acorn might mean. She'd gone God knew where, and she'd done it deliberately.

He wanted to scream, to yell across the mountain until she heard him and came back. He wanted to tell her that he didn't care about the fairies, or the voices, or whatever the hell they were. Tell her he'd never felt more real than when he was with her, that he'd never held anyone as tenderly as he had her last night. Tell her he didn't want her to go.

He hunched down, doubled with a pain that wasn't physical. A helicopter droned, familiar from Belfast on a troubled night. It hovered over the big glen opposite.

That got him to his feet. He needed to get to the house and Mark, and get the search moved to the right place.

Even as he thought that, he took in the bleak landscape around him: hill after hill joined by a network of small roads. Rivers criss-crossed the land, sometimes wide, sometimes narrow enough to cross. By the time he'd got down the hill and called for help, she could be into the next glen and buried in the land. Searching for her was important, yes, but he and Mark had searched for her at the waterfall and hadn't found her. He remembered Mark's words from that night – if Amy didn't want to be found, she wouldn't be. He needed to do more than search: he had to figure out what she might do next.

He skidded down, trying to hurry but not banjax his ankle completely, replaying everything he knew about her. She'd go where it was safe, especially if she was scared. He glared at the bleak hill. In the distance, the incessant sea beat its way to land and out again. He turned away, his gaze flitting from one field to another. He hated this place, but he no longer had the option of taking the bus out of the glens and back to Belfast: not until she was found. The land had taken him by taking Amy.

AMY STOPPED AT the sound of laughter carrying through the air. It was so different from the fairies' high voices – a proper laugh, throaty and familiar: Tori, the only person guaranteed to raise a smile no matter how bad things were. She stumbled along the rutted path, and her friend appeared a few feet in front of her, coming and going, at once sharp then blurred.

Tori held up her phone, and Amy recognised the Marvel casing, scrawled over with Tori's graffitti. "Did you get the picture?"

Amy smiled. She knew what Tori meant: her proof-Amy's-not-mad-picture of Britney Spears during her meltdown, cutting all her hair off. Until Amy did the same, Tori had told her, she wasn't too bad. That caught the edge of her panic. She had been so much better, for so long. A choked sob grew in her throat.

"You've still got your hair! You're okay!" yelled a Tori who couldn't possibly be there. A Tori who'd stuck with Amy through every mad episode, who was one of the few friends her mother hadn't managed to drive away. A Tori Amy wanted to get to, very much.

"Situation normal," agreed Amy, but she didn't know if Tori had heard her. Her friend faded. Amy ran forwards, slipping and sliding, hands out. If Tori gave up on her, what was left?

She stumbled to where Tori had been and stopped. Her friend was gone. Amy was lost in the middle of nowhere, imagining people, her head swimming with dizziness, her leg a knot of pain each time she put weight on it. Situation anything but normal.

She took a moment to get her bearings. The hill she'd climbed yesterday, the one with the cairn, loomed not far away, sending a chill through her. Singing started, low and familiar. Icy fingers touched her spine, a reminder of the previous day.

She could not let it happen again. She stared ahead, focusing on anything that wasn't the voices: the soft cheep of nearby birds; the lowing of a cow somewhere on the hill; a long bleat from a sheep.

"Right then." She pushed her damp hair back from her forehead, aware of the heat of her wrist. She didn't have time to waste.

With effort, she turned away from the hill and the song. The singing grew louder, pulling at the fey part of her, but she trudged through the mud, determined not to turn back. A line of grey cut through the green, and she realised it was the road. She sped up, hissing at the pain in her leg. The voices grew shrill.

Don't listen. She imagined Simon in front of her, telling her that she could ignore them.

"You don't know what it's like." She sounded like a child, petulant and sulky. She slipped in a puddle but kept going, hot one moment, cold the next. She reached a gate and climbed over, coming out on the road. A sign opposite swayed in the light breeze, half hidden by trees. More holiday cottages; every farmer in the Glens must be at it. Houses meant phones, and civilisation. People, not fairies. She scrambled across the road and the voices calling from the cairn dropped away, giving blessed relief.

She reached the bottom of a steep drive and climbed it until she came to a car park, with a single car, beside a terrace of modern cottages. A hedgerow framed the car park, splitting it from a field of sheep including a ram with the biggest balls she'd ever seen. She made the mistake of imagining what Tori might say, snorted, and felt slightly astonished that she could find anything funny about the situation.

The sound of accompanying laughter took her attention away from her sudden humour. A group of young fairies sat on the lowest branch of a nearby hawthorne tree. Their hair fell to their shoulders in a golden shower, their wings, long and pointed, shimmered in the rising sunlight. She reached out and one fluttered onto her hand, so soft she barely felt a tickle.

The fairy bowed; *Amy, Amy, our Amy.* It did a dance, gave a tinkling giggle and vanished. Amy closed her hand over where it had been – surely no fantasy could be so real.

To compound the proof of reality, the other fairies were

still in the tree, all golden happiness. One held her hand out and beckoned. She looked like Tori; Tori who'd never wanted anything but the best for Amy.

But looking closer, Amy could see its eyes were too sharp and watchful. Its ears pricked and attentive. Amy could not call for help without the fairies knowing. The world spun. Her plan – to call Mark and get him to come for her – would not work. Her legs threatened to give under her. Everything that had driven her to this point vanished – as long as the fairies were with her, no help would make any difference. She was trapped – and they knew it.

CHAPTER EIGHTEEN

THE SOUND OF drumming, followed by over-zealous splashing, woke Mark. He rolled onto his back with a low groan. What a night. The kicking had been bad enough, but he'd cried, to his father of all people, like a snotty nosed teen who couldn't cope. Jesus. He remembered the pub, the sharp knowledge of what he'd wanted, how he'd brought the beating on himself, whiskey-coated. *That* he could stand, but not the loss of control.

He sat up and winced at the sharp line of pain along his abdomen. The bed next to him was empty, the covers thrown back; his dad was up before midday, a minor miracle in itself.

The sound of water stopped. Mark got up and pulled on his clothes, and waited on the edge of the bed. Better to get seeing his dad over with. Then he'd only have to face his mother. *That* wouldn't be pretty.

The bathroom door opened and his dad emerged, freshly-shaven, hair brushed back and neat in a pony-tail, albeit one with the familiar red postie-band. But it wasn't just his appearance; something in the set of his shoulders took Mark back years, to when they were kids, before the little glen when Amy had gone missing and everything had changed. His lips stung as he broke into a smile.

"Welcome back," he said. "I thought you were never coming out from under that hair."

His dad smiled, and it crinkled the corner of his eyes, like he meant it. "I hope I can stay back this time." He cracked his knuckles. "Back to Monday evenings at the community centre, I guess." He sobered, his dark eyes reflective, and glanced out of the window.

Mark followed his look and took in the rugged hills beyond, the glens spreading all the way across the horizon, empty and huge, and he understood. His dad might have found the strength he needed to be a proper father, but for Amy, it might be too late.

"Mark." Dad's voice was quiet, but firm. "There's something I think you should know." He sat on the bed opposite. "Something about your mum – it might make it all easier to understand."

Understanding would be good. "Shoot."

"Before I met your mother, I knew some of this. Most people in the area did, it was the talk of the place." He ran his hands up and down his thigh, as if not sure where to start, and then gave a small shrug. "You're not her first child."

"What?" He didn't know what he'd expected, but it hadn't been that. "I have a brother, or sister? Where?" And why didn't he know?

His father shook his head. "The baby died. Soon after birth. Your mother was still at school. She said she didn't know she was pregnant before she had the baby."

"How could she not know?" Mark mimed a bump with his hands. "I mean, it's sort of obvious, no?"

"I think we were a bit more naïve than your generation." Dad gave a gentle smile. "To be honest, I expect she *did* know, but didn't know how to tell anyone. Could you imagine telling your Gran you were in that position? In the late-seventies, in Belfast?"

Mark winced. His gran might be two years dead but the memory of her was still fresh: her forthright views, her way of cutting a person down with two words. No, he couldn't imagine finding a way to tell her.

"How old was Mum?" He was surprised how hoarse his voice was.

"Fifteen. It was with a long-term boyfriend." Dad's face twisted. "Who scarpered as fast as he could when it all came out."

"So, what happened? To the baby, I mean." The brief, hideous thought crossed his mind that it might have something to do with Gran, but he smothered it. She'd been hard work, for sure, the definition of a battle axe, but he'd never believe she could do something to a baby.

"It was born in the bathroom in the middle of the night." Dad leaned forward. "Imagine that – giving birth on your own, in a bathroom, at fifteen."

Mark shivered. "It must have been horrific."

"So it's always sounded – from everyone who was there. The baby was fine, but a bit small. Your mum and him were taken to the Royal. A week later, she was sent home. Three days after that, the baby died."

"Why?" Mark couldn't believe no one had ever told him this before, that his family could have something like this buried and him not know. "Was he sick?"

"That's the tricky bit." Dad paused, as if sorting through his memories. "Remember, I got most of this second hand. The general wisdom was that the baby was sickly right from the start. He might have been hurt during the birth, or that your mum might have starved him trying not to let herself get too fat."

"I can see that." His mother, the ultimate controller. If she'd known she was pregnant and had been determined to hide it, starving herself was entirely possible. But what had she hoped to do with the baby? Perhaps she thought, once it was out, her own mother would have to accept how things were. Certainly she'd have had no other choice but to carry the baby to term. It was hard enough to get an abortion these days – before cheap flights made it possible to get to England and back in a day, it would have been close to impossible.

"Your mother couldn't. She wouldn't tell anyone what she thought had happened to the baby. The rumours were she'd hurt him herself, either through an accident, or …" He gave a shrug. "You can join the dots."

"What do you think?" Surely his mother, no matter how bad things were, wouldn't have hurt her own baby. And yet, he thought of the cold woman of the last few months, and had to fight a shiver in his spine.

"I don't think she hurt Matthew." His dad sounded sure. "She loved him to bits – she obsessed about him for years. No, she always said someone – not her – had hurt him." He looked back out the window, his eyes raking the glens. Finally, he looked back at Mark. "She believed it so much she was hospitalised for a year."

Jesus. It put a new emphasis on everything that had happened the last few months. Had Amy turning eighteen felt like his mother was losing all her children?

"Like Amy?" he asked. A mental illness, he could face. He'd lived with Amy's obsessions over the years; he thought he could accommodate his mother's, if he had to.

A firm shake of his dad's head. "No, not like Amy. Your mother's beliefs presented as an undoubted psychosis. Amy's knows the fairies might not be real. Your mother has never stopped believing the baby died because of something sinister, something she would never tell anyone." He held his hands out. "She didn't want any more children, not for a long time."

"In case it happened again."

"Yes. It took me years to convince her we could keep our children safe." His eyes met Mark's. "And then Amy disappeared."

It all fell into place. The obsessive questioning of Amy, the incessant need to know about the fairies, what Amy had seen, what they'd said. His mother had been scanning for threats, seeking any truth that might convince her things were okay and safe. Perhaps, in believing the fairies were real, it made them a threat that could be talked about and faced.

He remembered the first time Amy had been treated, the murmured conversations between his parents, the fear she might hurt herself, that she'd get worse, the stories read from the paper about teenagers committing suicide. An imaginary threat had to be easier to face than the real one. Especially when his mother already knew what mental illness felt like, when she'd already experienced its long drop out of normality. He swallowed past the lump in his throat. What a mess. "Poor Mum."

"Yes," said his dad, "poor Mum. And even poorer

because she doesn't want sympathy for it. Perhaps we should have told you before, but... when was the time? Not when you were a child. And how would Amy feel, realising how what was happening to her must be affecting her mum? We were so busy trying to play it down, convincing Amy it was just a phase. What if she thought that she had something hereditary that was never going to go away? So it got left unsaid and buried, and I suppose – we hoped it had gone away."

"Jesus." Who was going to tell Amy when she got back?

"Anyway ... your mum?" Dad's eyes were pleading. "Be kind to her, eh? Throw her a bit of forgiveness?"

Be kind to her? His father hadn't been kind to his mother the night before; he'd fought the peace out with her.

"Like you are?" Mark's words weren't as sharp as they should be. "You're asking me to do something you can't do yourself."

His father nodded and his eyes were sadder than Mark had ever seen.

"I tried." His throat rippled. "God knows I tried. But in the end it got too much – she wore me down, blaming me for convincing her to have children, pushing me away." He got to his feet. "I wish things weren't the way they are, I wish I could comfort her, but she stopped seeking it from me a long time ago."

"You could try again," said Mark. "You're sober this morning, you're more like yourself."

His father nodded, and he really did look like the father of his childhood. "You're right. I'll try too." He grimaced. "One day at a time, isn't that what they say?" He'd been to more than his share of AA meetings over the years. Usually the first one and no more. "Let's get everyone through this day, to Amy being found, eh? After, we can pick up the pieces. Deal?"

Mark nodded. It sounded good. It even sounded like it might be possible. "Deal."

Chapter Nineteen

A MY CREPT ALONG a narrow path behind the houses, skirting what looked like a storm gully, and stopped dead at the dull click of a door being unlocked. She shrank back as the door of the single house with its curtains drawn swung open to reveal an occupant.

"Come on, Bones." A man, perhaps in his forties, dressed for the chill morning in a beaten-up wax jacket, waited for an equally-scruffy dog to come out. He closed the door carefully, as if not wanting to make too much noise, but didn't lock it – given the remoteness of the cottage and earliness of the day, he probably didn't see the need. After a quiet click of his tongue, the dog trotted behind him.

Amy waited until they were out of sight before she crept along the pebble-filled gully, and tip-toed into the small yard. Breath held, she listened by the back door. All was quiet – no voices or television. She looked through a crack in the curtains and saw a small kitchen area and larger living room. Both were empty. She thought back to how carefully the man had closed the door and decided it was likely the rest of the household were still asleep.

A stroke of luck, or something else? The fairies from the hawthorne tree had followed her and were gathered around the door, waiting for her.

She glanced at her battered sandals and ragged dress. A headache throbbed behind her eyes. She needed clothes and food. Everything appeared too sharp, shifted about, as if she had already half left the world. Perhaps the fairies wouldn't take her in some wild manner, but let her fade into their world instead. The way she felt, fading would be a relief.

Okay, then, showtime. She shook out her arms, building herself up. If she was caught, the residents would call the police for sure. She put her hand on the door-handle, still listening. It opened smoothly onto an open plan kitchen and living area, bare of anything useful. She slipped off her sandals and crept across the room to stand beside an ajar door that must lead to the hallway beyond. She could make out the muffled noise of a radio or TV, but nothing else. No thuds to indicate anyone was moving around.

Even so, she needed to be quick. She spun round and saw another door next to the back entrance. She slipped across, making little noise on the wooden floor, and tried the door, which opened into a small cloakroom.

Perfect. She rifled through the coats until she found a denim jacket, a bit big, but it would do. Her gaze lighted on a row of shoes below. All the adult ones looked too big for her, but a pair of kid's trainers, decorated with glittered butterflies and flowers, were promising enough to pull out. She turned them over. The soles had roses imprinted in deep lines – at least they'd have a decent grip. They looked to be about the right size, and she eased her feet into them, wincing. She took a couple of steps. They were a bit small, but bearable and definitely better than her sandals.

What else? She crept into the kitchen and pulled open the door of the washer-dryer. She discarded a man's t-shirt and pulled out the most glorious dress, mint-green picked out with pink roses, cut in an empire line. She rubbed its soft fabric, but jumped at a noise behind her, sure it was the man with the dog or someone from upstairs.

Three female fairies fluttered in a row around shoulder-height. They had the look of teenagers about them, in the way they kept their bodies closed off from each other, in their self-conscious eyes. They were looking at the dress in utter adoration, their wings shimmering as they hovered, hands clasped.

Amy closed her eyes, counted to five, and opened them again. The fairies were still there, and very, very real. She held up the dress. "You like?"

They liked. She tugged off her rag of a dress and put the new dress on. It was a little short, and held the lingering scent of someone else's perfume, but not bad. With the jacket over it she looked decent. Or at least not so odd someone would comment.

She took a moment to raid the kitchen cupboards and came out triumphant with a round of bread. Her headache throbbed and her vision went odd – not quite an aura, but threatening to become one – so that she smeared jam on the back of her hand instead of the bread. It looked like blood. She took a bite of the bread and moaned with relief, devouring the rest of it in about three bites. Her headache receded.

"Now what?" she asked. Since the fairies were here, wanting her attention, they might as well be useful. They spun in a twirl of wings and blossom that fell onto the floor and melted away as if it'd never been there. The scent of spring filled the room, cutting through the deep mellowness of early autumn. They flitted to the door and waited.

"Come with you?" she asked. With determination, she kept her voice steady. "Where to?"

To free you.

That wasn't enough; she needed to know more. "Where?"

No doubts; no doubts; just you. Their faces grew distorted. Their teeth grew longer. Their golden hair dulled. Their mouths drew back into snarls as their voices hit her, no giggling golden fairies now, but harder. She tried to turn away, but they surrounded her, faces close to her, sharp, sharp teeth bared; Tori's face made different, a mask of friendship torn away.

There were more than three fairies now. At least ten, all around her. She put her hand out, steadying herself against the counter, and touched a knife on the sideboard. It was cold under her palm and she wanted to recoil from it, but her hand tightened around it, her fingers commanded by something she couldn't fight. She knew what they wanted it for; the murderous intent sparkled in the air, its focus on Simon. They *were* taking her back to the glens, then, where he might be waiting for her.

"I can't walk any further," she told them. Please, let it work. "I need the car."

A fairy dropped onto a handbag sitting on the next chair with a solid thud. A woman's voice floated from upstairs, calling for Gary.

Open it, the fairies said. She did, searching until she felt the hard edges of a set of car keys, and hooked them from the bag.

"Gary!" the voice called again, followed by the bump of someone getting up and crossing their room upstairs.

The fairies held the bag for Amy. She had no time to spare. *Yes*, they said, and she understood. Today they had called her for the last time. They'd take her to a place of their choosing and steal her from the world. Nothing would stop them, not her tiredness or fear.

The thump of feet on the stairs made the fairies agitated. They moved to the door, urging her to be quick, to come with them now. A group of them broke away, gathering around the door from the hallway. She opened the back door. "Come on."

She ran around the house, into the car park with its single car. The man and his dog weren't in sight. The fairies helped her to the car, half-lifting her off her feet, stronger than they looked.

It was huge, a people carrier. It was bad enough stealing a car, but not one this size – she'd barely managed to drive Mark's MINI.

The teenage fairies pulled at her clothes. *Come, come, come; we'll help, come, come.* Seductive voices, loud and getting louder, making her headache worse, so that the ground spun and wavered and she couldn't stay on her feet. She pressed the key fob until one of the buttons caused a pulse of headlights from the car, and she pulled open the driver's door.

The fairies streamed past her, delighted. They were the delinquents of the fairy world, she decided. They took up positions all through the car, some on the backseat, one on the dashboard, a few lined up along the luggage-shelf in the boot. The dashboard-fairy looked at her intently and pointed out the front window. *Go, go, go*. The door slammed closed.

Amy set the knife on the passenger seat with sticky hands. She held her palm out to the fairy on the dashboard, who hopped onto it, wings fluttering in gossamer threads. Her feet shifted on Amy's hand, a beat-beat dance. The voices might not be real, but the drumming on her fingers and the wind from the wings couldn't be faked. Amy lowered her hand and the fairy danced back onto the dashboard.

Go, go, go. In the mirror, the woman from the house had rounded the corner of the building, a phone to her ear.

Amy stuck the key in the ignition. She'd only completed three lessons – three long-awaited lessons, only granted after her doctor's sign-off – before Mark had bailed out and told her he was never, ever, getting into a car again with her. Absolutely mental, he'd called her: a liability. He'd been white as a sheet. And it had only been a little kerb.

She turned the key and the car jumped forward. Shit, shit, shit. Neutral, it had to be in neutral. She put the gear-stick into the middle, started the car, and managed to find reverse. There was a lurch and she barely turned the wheel before the car hit the house. The woman reeled back, her face white and shocked.

Amy teetered on the edge of her seat, so she was practically standing, and chose first gear. The wheels spun and the car shot forwards. The courtyard wall was worryingly close from this angle. She wrenched the wheel to the side, and somehow managed to get the car through the gates and onto the steep driveway. She was going too fast. The fairy on the dashboard looked terrified.

"Oh, shit!" She pressed the brake pedal, and the car stalled to a halt. Maybe Mark had a point. There was no way she could do this. She thudded her head onto the steering wheel and reached for the door. The fairies gathered around her, yammering at her to try again. One sat on the door lock. *Oh, God, this was crazy.* Her hand shook as she reached for the key, and turned it.

"Right," she muttered. The car lurched onto the road. To her right, the man ran towards her, dog lolloping beside him. He shouted something, but she ignored him, getting into second gear and then third. She followed the road to a junction and paused to read the signs. The country road looked much like another – in these parts the difference between these almost-empty lanes and the tourist-filled Coast Road was marked.

The fairies got excited, as if on a day-trip. They were passing sweets between them, for heaven's sake, and took turns to flutter up to the window. If she turned right she'd go deeper into the glens, away from the coast.

She wanted to finger her neck, bared of her pendant, but instead tightened her hands on the steering wheel and, with all the will she had left in her, wrenched the wheel to the left. She would go to the place of her own choosing, where she'd be safe from them.

The fairies did nothing to stop her, and she didn't stop to wonder why.

CHAPTER TWENTY

MARK FOLLOWED HIS dad to the breakfast room. His mother waited by the bay window, her face pinched and worried, her eyes far away as they scanned the empty landscape beyond. He wished he could reach out and tell her he finally understood, but his father was right. After they found Amy, he could confront the past. Not today when the fear was raw that Amy might not come back, and his mother would be left with just him, a useless replacement for her children lost to the fairies.

"Hello, Mum." She didn't turn as he approached and he put his hand on her shoulder. "It'll be okay. We'll find her."

She spun to him, ready, he guessed, to challenge him, but her hand went to her mouth. "What happened to you?"

He glanced at his dad, who shrugged; he'd already said he wouldn't be explaining the fight.

"I ran into some locals I should have avoided." Let that be enough – his own hang-ups could also wait. "It looks worse than it is."

His mum stepped closer, her eyes narrowed, and his

chest tightened, half in fear, half in hope. Did she know what he'd done and why? He'd been sure she did, last time it had happened. But if she did, his mother never responded. He didn't know if she understood, or if it even mattered.

She put her hand against his cheek, just under his partially-closed eye. He flinched and told himself it was because her hand was cold, but her palm felt warm against his skin. He was afraid of who she'd become, this mother a million miles from the one of his childhood, who'd built dens in the woods and made fun, odd meals to use up mismatched contents from the fridge. He glanced at his dad and saw the warning in his eyes. He might understand things more but it didn't make it any easier to reach her.

They stood for a long moment, her hand on his cheek, his breath held. He couldn't have said if he wanted the moment to last or to break, crystal-sharp, just as their relationship had.

"You should be more careful." She dropped her hand. Her eyes were cold, uncaring. No telling him not to get into fights, no pushing to know more. His breath left him in a whoosh. He hated himself for caring but he couldn't switch off the loving childhood, even if she seemed to have. He reached for her, ready to try to bridge the gulf between them.

The sound of low voices came from the hall, and the moment passed. The police officers from yesterday came into the room. He gulped, trying to read their faces, but couldn't.

"Officers." His dad nodded a greeting, his nod firmer than his voice. "Have you found Amy? Or the lad?"

"No." The male officer looked deeply uncomfortable, but he cleared his throat and went on, "We have a search underway. The volunteer rescue teams are out as well, and the helicopters." He looked between them, each in turn. "We are doing everything we can to find your daughter."

The female officer guided Mum to a seat. "I'm afraid, however, that this has become a criminal case."

Mark's heart stuttered. "What –?"

Dad found his voice first. "In what way?" The words were tight; fearful.

"We believe Amy stole a car."

Mark almost laughed, he was so relieved. Amy was no thief.

"There must be a mistake," his mum said.

"Amy wouldn't do that." Dad was adamant.

"She can barely drive in a straight line," said Mark. It seemed a salient point.

"I'm afraid there is little doubt," said the police-woman. She had drawn her legs together, almost primly. Obviously a sick, missing girl required different empathy than a criminal. "A farmer saw someone matching her description this morning, near some holiday houses, shortly before the car was stolen from them. It's hard to imagine too many other eighteen-year-olds running around the glens at dawn in a party dress." She put her hat on. "We need to ask that you stay here." She glanced at all three of them, each in turn, as if daring them to argue. "We need to know where to find you."

Sit and do nothing? It made no sense, not when they'd need everybody possible to search for Amy. Especially if she did have a car – there was a lot of ground to be covered, and his parents and him knew the fae places Amy might find, as she always did.

A sharp glance from his father made him swallow his

protests.

"Sure," Dad said. "That's fine." He gave a broad smile, as if hoping to placate. "But, for the record, it must be a mistake."

"Until we find her, we're keeping an open mind."

Mark frowned. It sounded like the police had the very opposite of open minds. The officers said their goodbyes and headed out the door, the clunk of it hitting the frame very final in the quiet room.

"It can't have been her," said Dad, shaking his head.

But it *might* have been, Mark admitted silently to himself. When Amy was off on one of her jaunts, she was impossible to predict.

"We need to find her," said Mark. That was the important thing – ending things today, before they got worse. "Where would she go?"

"Give me a haystack and a needle." His dad started to pace and Mark knew a day of watching him eat the carpet was more than he could face.

"The police can't cover all the glens." Although now it was a criminal matter, they might be more enthused about the search. He didn't point that out. "I say we go look for her."

His dad looked pleased at the prospect of something to do. He nodded at Mum. "Emma? Do you want to come?"

"The police said we should stay."

"Then stay. I'm going out to find our daughter, not leave her abandoned on a mountain." His words were too sharp, and Mum's face turned pinched and angry. So much for being kind to her.

"Saint Phil to the rescue," she said. "Lucky Amy, having *you* to rely on."

Oh, for Christ's sake, off they went again. Mark put his hands up. "Guys. Leave it, eh?"

His dad gave a sharp nod, ready to back down, but Mum came forwards, practically bristling.

"You stay off the drink for one night and suddenly you're Mr-I-don't-abandon-my-kids," she said. "You abandoned them years ago. I've held those kids together while you buggered off to your boat. Don't tell me about letting anyone down…"

"Enough!" His dad's hands clenched and for a moment Mark thought he might actually hit Mum, but he managed to unclench them. "Did you ask your son why he was stupid enough to take a kicking last night?"

"Dad, stop." This wasn't helping. "Let's go and look for Amy. That's what we care about, right?"

His mum's gaze flitted from place to place, glassy and unfocused. The time Amy had vanished in the little glen she'd been like this. Adamant she was right, talking no sense, and listening to none either.

"We shouldn't interfere," she said. "It's not our place."

Mark put his hand on her shoulder, squeezing gently. "Mum, Amy's sick." He said it the way the doctors did, as a statement of fact. He looked straight into her eyes. "I know you've humoured her about the fairies, but it's time to stop. She's not well. And she's on her own."

"The doctors can't tell us what it is. None of their drugs have worked." She held her hands out, as if pleading for belief. "I *know* what's wrong." Her eyes shone with conviction. "Neither of you understand."

"Emma…" Dad said, his voice a low warning. "We can argue about what is or isn't causing things later. If you want to stay here and wait, that's fine. I could drive your car."

Something flitted across her face, something cold, almost calculating, chilling Mark. It fell away quickly, replaced by a mask of a smile. "There's no way in hell's Earth you're driving my car." She handed Mark the keys. "I'll see you out there; I need the toilet. Wait for me."

She left, leaving Mark to stare after her, trying to place why the smile had so unsettled him. He followed his dad out into what was, at least, a better day, with some late-summer sun threatening. He couldn't remember being up this early on a Sunday morning in ages; normally he'd be sleeping in to avoid facing another day off. His enforced exile had, if nothing else, brought home to him how shit his life was, how much of it revolved around his family and Amy. Last night, talking to his dad and admitting he'd sought out a beating to make him feel alive had made his emptiness undeniable. Someone normal would have had a person to call – a friend, if not a girlfriend – to tell them how crap things were.

As soon as they found Amy and consigned this weekend to another crazy-Amy anecdote, he'd do something about it. Look up some of his old friends, take up the offers of nights out with work. Anything to widen his life, and give him a chance to find Mark, not Mad Amy's brother.

If they found Amy. He swallowed the quick flash of fear. If the police were right, she'd been out and about that morning. He pulled open the passenger door, forcing his dad into the back. At least his parents would have to make an effort to fight.

"God, my head feels like it's going to burst," said his dad, getting in. "That policeman this morning – what he was saying about Amy. If it was her, she must be ... disturbed." Mad, crazy, listening to the voices. This time, something would have to be done about it. She wasn't a wee girl, able to be kept close and safe. She had a life of her own, was at college – somehow a solution would have to be found.

His dad rubbed his head, and Mark could see how his fingers were digging into his skin, as if he could burrow in and find the answers he needed. The damage the years had done to their family seemed to be written in every line of his face. Perhaps, for his dad, finding Amy mattered more than to anyone else. He'd been the one who'd walked away – he'd have to live, knowing she might never learn he'd come to find her. That she'd believed he was the drunken sot he had been for years.

"We will. Half of Ulster's looking for her." But the words were weak, even to Mark's ears. Half of Ulster wouldn't make a dent in the sort of hiding Amy could do.

"Hardly, given the population around here." Dad's mouth twisted. "Half of Ulster's sheep, maybe. Unless they're bringing people up from Belfast." He craned his neck towards the guesthouse. "Where the hell is your mum?"

"She's coming." His mum closed the door of the lodge behind her, and hurried to the car, her steps quick, almost jaunty. She swung her legs into the driver's seat. A wave of her familiar perfume hit Mark, spicy and dangerous. That, combined with the briskness of her taking the keys off him and the flashing smile she gave, made it seem as if the last horrid months had disappeared and she'd come back to herself.

"You'll never believe what just happened." She started the car. "May just took a call. Someone saw a wee girl on her own, up near some hidden village deep in the Glens. Who has the map?"

"I do." Mark pulled it out of his top pocket and unfolded it. He read the map's information panel and found mention of the deserted village. There were stories of hermits living there. He passed it back to his dad, who smiled broadly. It was exactly the sort of place Amy would make for.

They took the inland road, climbing quickly into the heart of the glens-land. The landscape changed from remote to empty. The road narrowed to the point where his mum hunched over the wheel, concentrating on each twist and turn. The car's small engine protested, over-revving as she had to slip down a gear. At last, soon after Mark was sure he and his dad were going to have to get out and push, they pulled into a small car park beside a ruined church. There were no other cars.

"May said we could walk up from here," said his mum. "Easier this way, apparently."

"This is pretty bleak," Mark said as he got out. His unease from earlier came back, that sense of a missing meaning. Something important. It nagged at him, just at the edge of his thoughts, not possible to grasp.

The small church wasn't much more than a ruin, with no roof and one end wall fallen into rubble. Two trees stood either side of a dilapidated gateway, as if standing guard. He strode into the churchyard and followed a moss-covered path, past graves, crooked like old men's teeth, to a tree hung with rags of clothing, old and knotted. He touched one of the rags.

His dad joined him. "A rag-tree," he said. "People put the cloths there in memory of the dead."

Mark let the cloth go, pulling his hand back as if burned. The wind shifted the rags. He fought not to peer deeper into the shadows all around, cast by the trees.

He turned on his heel, away from the tree and the thoughts of death. "Amy! It's Mark!"

His dad followed and they took their time, calling and calling for her, but received only eerie silence in reply. The churchyard was still; waiting, watching. The sun scudded behind a cloud, casting the day into cold darkness. Had Amy been here? He couldn't tell. "Amy!" His voice carried over the glens, up to the sky, and no answer came.

The path took him to the back of the church, where his mum had made her way to from the other side of the building. Part of the wall had fallen, leaving a gap to walk though, with a path snaking up the hill.

"I suppose that's the way," he said.

"Must be." His mum had that smile again, with the little twist that made it seem both familiar and new.

"It looks like private land." His dad had joined them. He looked up the path doubtfully. "Would she have got this far? There was no other car at the church."

"There must be other places to pull in," said his mum. "The village isn't at the church, it's a bit further on."

"She got up a glen in the dark," said Mark. "If she really did steal a car I suppose she might have come this way. Unless she cra –" He stopped himself just in time; the image of Amy lying somewhere off the B-road in a heap of tangled metal would help no one. Besides, something of his lessons must have sunk in if she'd even managed to start the bloody thing. "How sure was May that it *was* her?"

"She said the description matched." His mum stepped forward, decisively. "Besides, the police are looking in all the obvious places."

His dad climbed over the remains of the wall. They exchanged a look, and Mark gave a careful nod. It was a lead, which was more than they had anywhere else. He started to climb the hill.

It wasn't until he was well up it, the church out of sight and lost, that he realised when he'd seen his mother's smile before. The night of the wedding, when she'd left Amy and went back to Belfast. The night Amy had finally, after years of battling the voices, succumbed. The night it all started.

Chapter Twenty-One

THE ROAD CAME into sight. Simon, breathing heavily, picked out the farmyard, its three barns shining in the sunshine, but no movement. He had no idea how long it had taken to find his bearings – too long – and then to make his way down the hill, panic leaping in his throat at the minutes ticking by. Twice he'd seen a helicopter – both times it had been too far away for him to draw its attention.

He reached the road, glad to feel the flat, smooth surface underfoot. He jogged, starting and stopping according to his ankle's protest and began to get his breath back from the sheer hurtle downhill. He made his way to the little cottage. The lack of cars outside the cottage made the yard feel too empty.

He banged on the outside door, but no one answered. A glance through the window of the breakfast room showed only empty seats and tables laid for the next serving. Where had Mark gone?

He made his way over the farmhouse and paused in front of the door, hands wringing one another. He shook them out, collecting himself. Even if the news was bad, he had to know. He knocked on the door and waited, shoving his hands into his pocket, where they couldn't betray him. His fingertips grazed the acorn, and he turned it between his fingers. From inside he could hear the thud of doors closing, a television loud and then muffled. His stomach made a good attempt to climb into his throat.

The door opened. May's face broke into a wide smile. "Heavens, you're in one piece." She all but pulled him down a shabby hallway to a cavernous, stone-flagged kitchen, its casual comfort a mile away from the formality of the B&B's dining room. Warmth from an AGA hit him. He sank onto one of the chairs at the table. He had to ask but the words were stuck in his throat.

"Did you stumble across the wee girl?" she asked. Her words sent a sharp shard though him, telling him what he needed to know. Amy was still alone somewhere, wandering the glens. A chill ran through him, bone-deep; assuming she *was* still wandering, and nothing worse had happened. May set a cup of steaming coffee in front of him. "The police are searching for her."

"I found her," he said. "We spent the night in a shed."

"Mercy me. On a night like that, if you hadn't found shelter, you'd be dead of exposure." She looked over his shoulder, eyes confused. "Where is she, then?"

"I don't know." His voice choked. "I haven't seen her today. Where's Mark?"

"Off searching for her. The mother said they had to do something to help. I tried to get her to stay, like the police wanted, but she said no."

So, Amy's mother had arrived. He should be relieved but his shoulders tightened, tense. She'd left the disco, knowing what Amy might be seeing. Worse, if what Amy had said had any truth – if her mother really *did* believe in the fairies – she'd left knowing they might be real.

He wanted to hit the table in frustration. He needed to talk to Mark and find out how sick Amy really was. He needed the family to get up the mountain and find her. They could convince her to come in and be treated – they'd done so in the past.

May thudded a bowl of soup in front of him.

"Get some of that into you." She handed him a spoon. "I'll call the police. They might be able to work out where you were." Her lips pursed. "Although I think they know where she is, or where's she's been." Her voice dropped, conspiratorially. "She stole a car."

Oh, Christ; things were just going from better to worse. Amy could be anywhere, and, once lost, she'd be able to stay lost.

May left. He waited until he heard her talking on the phone and then pushed the soup away, not able to face it. He looked around; as if seeking inspiration; as if Amy might suddenly materialise. His eyes fell on the familiar jumble of his phone and wallet on the windowsill. Had it only been a day ago when he'd left them in the guesthouse?

May was still talking, her voice droning on, no doubt drawing out his story. The police would scare the life out of Amy. He put his head in his hands, massaging his temples. If she had a car where would she go? Out of the Glens, towards Belfast and safety? His head came up, working it out. Safety. Suddenly, he knew where to go.

May's voice had started to rise, the way his mother's did when she was finishing off a call. Soon, the police would arrive with enough questions to last the afternoon. He got to his feet, moving the chair back quietly, grabbed his phone, and left.

Chapter Twenty-Two

A MY PASSED A sign welcoming her to Cushendun and found herself smiling. She could just make out the little ice-cream shop, its shopfront lined with buckets and spades and the café she and Mark had visited each day for cake.

She stopped the car at the head of the harbour. Straight ahead took her over a bridge into the main village. Right led along the quayside to what looked like a dead end.

The caves lay beyond that dead end, in the maul of the cliffs. She put her foot on the accelerator, not understanding the flood of dread that filled her. The caves were her safe place. Once she got there, the nightmare would be over. She'd ask the first visitors for help. She'd take the medication the doctors told her to, she'd go back to hospital, she'd do whatever it took to never feel this way again.

A soft noise came from behind her, and she tensed. The fairies should be gone now she was here. Unlike with her necklace, which barely kept the voices at a distance, the caves had been empty of fairies. She'd stayed a full week, exploring with Mark, flitting back and forth from the caves, to the harbour, to the beach, and there hadn't been a single voice.

She steeled herself and glanced in the mirror. They weren't gone. They'd gathered in the back of the car, watching her. She stared at them, willing them to vanish, and heard the first whisper of new voices. Her stomach clenched. She shook her head to get rid of them but they grew louder until they were clear enough for her to make out: ancient voices, serious, not like the teenage mayhem-crew.

Keep going; we are waiting.

Unarguable with. She turned onto a narrow road, disassociated from her thoughts. Butterflies grew in her stomach, nauseating her. She drove slowly past apartments built into the lower levels of the cliff, past a statue of a goat overlooking the harbour for some unknown reason. Well-spaced bollards separated the harbour from the road. The boats lay slanted in the low tide. Lobster pots lined the quayside, propped against the bollards, making the available road even narrower. There was no way to turn back, nowhere to go but forward.

The road markings ended. A sharp turn to the right took her away from the harbour and past an electricity substation, its warnings of death highlighted: black on yellow. Her last feelings of safety evaporated. The public road became a causeway, passing between looming rocks, gnarled and old, as old as those in the circle. This was an ancient place, formed by nature and held by something that wasn't human. It was far from the haven it had once been, nestled in her dad's boat in the little harbour.

She drove slowly, forced into the middle of the

causeway, towards a dark cave-mouth, closer than she remembered. Whilst the individual rocks were huge, the cave system was surprisingly compact, almost claustropbic.

Rocks, easily the height of the car, hemmed her in on the left. She glanced in the mirror. The fairies were watching, eyes sharp. One smiled, not a nice smile. She felt sick at her own stupidity. This place was as fae as anywhere she'd ever been. The fairies knew her better than she knew herself. They knew that she had run when she was five, that she might always be strong enough to do what she had this morning and wrench the wheel to the side. They'd known to trap her.

How old had she been on the boat-holiday? Her parents hadn't officially split but they'd been close to it – in truth, it had been the beginning of the end. Fourteen, then. That had been the first year the voices had gained a hold on her: the year they'd changed tactics, had stopped enticing her with sugared images and had began talking to her, insinuating ideas, becoming stronger.

That had been the year her father had drawn away from the family. Without him to step in, her mother had begun to focus on the fairies. She'd started her whispering about what the fairies wanted and what Amy was to do.

She shuddered. The fairies had set this up, as staged as the show her mother had once taken her to in the park.

Her foot eased off the accelerator. If the fairies had gone to such trouble, there had to be something waiting for her. Something worse. The car glided to a stop.

She could reverse back to the main road, but was sure she'd end up crashing through the bollards and into the water. Her eyes widened at that; it mightn't be the worst thing. At least she'd have chosen it for herself. She put her foot on the accelerator but selected first gear, even as she tried to pull the stick into reverse. The car lurched forward, drawing nearer to the single dark cavern, following the lure of the old voices.

Tyre marks vanished into the darkness of the cave, and she followed them. The sunlight disappeared as the cave swallowed the car. Ahead, a set of barred double-gates in the rock mouth blocked the other end of the cave, but a driveway stretched beyond them, twisting to the left and out of sight. She stopped in front of the gates and peeled her fingers from the steering wheel.

Even if the police were looking for the car, they'd take a while to find it here. It was the perfect place for the fairies to have her alone. She let out a shallow, hissed breath.

The fairies in the car were still and alert. Waiting for events to unfurl, whatever they were. She stared out of the windscreen, trying to see through the shadows, but nothing moved. Whatever waited was patient. She looked behind her, judging how long it would take her to get to the village and help, but she'd have to go around the harbour. She'd be caught long before she made it.

Come. The first voice made her flinch with its sharpness. *Now, now, now.* She covered her ears with her hands, but it made no difference; she reached with fingers that didn't feel like her own, and opened the driver's door.

She stepped out. The air was dank, full of brine from the sea. The sound of waves echoed, surging and ebbing in rhythmic sucking breaths. Her breath followed as if she were a piece to the whole.

The teen fairies swooped around her, leading the way from the cave towards the harbour. They were everywhere and their voices never stopped, giving her no chance to catch her thoughts.

They led her into a short, stone-filled cove to the right, closed in on one side by the cliff, on the other by rocks, making an inverted triangle of blue sky and sea. Land in the distance – Scotland, presumably – was grey and ill-defined. There was no one in sight.

The teenage fairies had changed. In the car there'd been males and females of all shapes and sizes. Now, there were hundreds of them, all with dark, cropped hair, all female, all…. She stopped, barely breathing.

She had to be wrong. She looked again, taking her time to scrutinise. *They were all her*. She reached to touch one but it sprang away, its message clear; she was both of them, and separate. The air hardened around her, holding her tight; this place, whatever it was, wanted her.

Lucidity descended, forcing past her tiredness, shocking in its clarity. Fairies couldn't all look like her, it wasn't possible. And they couldn't know what Tori looked like, not unless they were inside her thoughts. She leaned on a rock for support. She'd stolen a car. What had she been thinking of? Her head thudded, dizzy and sick, and she shivered with a wash of cold sweat: she had no idea what to do. They'd never behaved like this. They'd always come to her, never trapped her like this. They'd never been so clever – or so determined.

Chapter Twenty-Three

"**Y**OU ALL RIGHT, mate?" The taxi driver's voice cut through Simon's thoughts; not a bad thing, given where they kept returning to.

"Aye." The car had joined the coast road, and a steady stream of traffic. He wanted to scream at the slow pace but settled for biting his nails instead. He was lucky to even have a cab – May had only called one when he'd threatened to walk to the nearest village if she didn't. "Why?"

"You look like you slept in a hedge."

Charming. Although the driver had a point. His once-new wedding suit had been ruined, its trouser hems covered in mud, a long, jagged tear over one knee. His shoes had lost any shape they'd ever had, his jacket was filthy from the shed, and his shirt had Amy's mascara smeared down it.

"It's been a long weekend," he said.

"Right." Simon didn't like something in the taxi-driver's voice, a knowing edge. He scanned the car and his eye fell on the newspaper on the well between the two seats, one he'd been doing his best to ignore since he'd been picked up for fear of drawing attention to his interest. Its headline screamed about a girl lost in the Glens. Simon could have cursed – damn the grapevine. News about Amy must have spread from kitchen to kitchen, over the telephone, through the little villages – whispered allegations that caught nothing of the truth.

"Is it you?" asked the taxi-driver.

Simon's knee jumped, but he managed to keep his voice steady. "Is what me?"

"The lad lost on the hills with the poor wee daft girl?"

Anger swelled and it was all he could do not to show it. Amy was anything but poor and wee. She'd been holding herself together for years, when most people would have given up long ago. He ignored the break of sweat across his shoulders. How long until word about the car theft was out and the driver felt the need to be helpful and report dropping him off? The one thing Amy didn't need was a police cell.

"A lad lost, too?" He gave a laugh, and doubted it would have convinced the village idiot. "What was he doing? Hunting fairies?"

They turned a corner and he spotted a sign: *Cushendun, 8 miles*. Twenty minutes to come up with some reason why he was here. A brown tourist sign flashed by, and he had a moment of divine, geek-filled inspiration.

"I'm going to see the caves." He leaned forward, letting his voice fill with excitement. "They were in Game of Thrones." Half the north coast had been used in the series; the locals must be used to all sorts turning up. "I told the lads to head back to Belfast – we had a quare night on the rag – and I'd go up and see them by myself."

"Never been before?" The taxi driver's tone changed

into what Simon expected was his best tourist guide's voice. "Spooky ol' place."

That made sense. His hand crept to his pocket and the acorn with its sharp edges. His finger traced the line of its crack. The back of his neck prickled. It felt like Amy could be right, that there was danger all around. He tightened his hand around the acorn and hoped it would be strong enough to protect them both.

AMY IGNORED THE double gate and instead dashed between a gap in the rocks to the left, into the pebbled inlet which led to the sea. From there she could clamber around to the harbour while the fairies were behind her and couldn't block her. It wasn't far, after all, not more than a few hundred yards.

She hurried, sliding and slipping, using her right hand to balance against the rocky wall. She misjudged a step, and yelped as her ankle twisted. She wrenched her foot free, ignoring the sharp pain. She could rest once she'd returned to civilisation. Not yet.

Amy reached the small shingle beach, its bare line of sand the last defence before the vast ocean. She didn't dare look behind her to see if the fairies had followed.

The sea was ahead of her, to the right of her, and encircling the small headland to her left. To reach the harbour she'd have to climb over the rocks that skirted the ocean. It would take too long, even if it was possible. A choked sob escaped her. One way in and one way out: the fairies knew she was trapped.

Waves surged towards her, strong from their journey

across the Atlantic. They echoed off the rocks with a boom, then a hiss as they dissolved into a white line of surf on the sand.

The hissing grew louder, closer. Amy turned. The mouth of the cove had filled with fairies. They approached, faces thin, mouths drawn back from sharp teeth, all glamour gone. She took a step back, the sea-smoothed pebbles clacking underfoot. She took another, and the first kiss of water touched her heel. Another, and it lapped her ankles, startling in its coldness. She had nowhere to go, except into the sea.

Look, look, look…

She turned again at their bidding. The sea swelled around her, pulling at her knees, carrying her forwards. The gash in her leg became a sharp burst of pain. She scanned the horizon but saw nothing except the line of sea meeting the sky. The last of the storm clouds were far out and the sun beat down, turning the surf into silver-lined foam. It rebounded from the rocks and cast salt motes in the sky. It reeked of the sea, briny and harsh. She licked it and it tasted like dulse seaweed, so salty it made her wince.

A wave splashed, waist-high, knocking her off balance. Hands on her back pushed her forwards, into the water, and she gasped at the cold. She tried to find her footing, thankful for the deep treads on her shoes. She thrust backwards, trying to stay near the beach, but fingers on her shoulders dug in, keeping her in the deeper water. They were so strong, not cute copies of Tori anymore, and had fingers like the branches of trees, hard and unyielding.

A noise to her right commanded her attention, a surging, sucking gush of intent. About fifty yards out, the hulk of an old ship had appeared. It listed at first, but straightened. Water escaped from under it, orange with rust.

Shapeless forms appeared, sharpening into elongated bodies of water. They reached up the sides of the boat with long hands.

Water-shee; she recognised them from Strangford Lough, when they'd led her off the edge of the pontoon and into the water. That was the day her father had finally called in the doctors, terrified she had tried to kill herself. She remembered waiting in his boat for the confirmation she'd finally lost her mind, Mark shivering in his wet clothes having jumped in after her. She'd thought things were bad then.

She ducked under the water, twisting her shoulders to escape, but the hands held her and she resurfaced, panting. The doctors said no one else saw the things she did, that they weren't real. But her imagination didn't have fingers. It didn't propel her through the water, to the boat, the current ripping around her legs as she powered forwards.

"No!" she shouted. Surely someone would hear her. The harbour wasn't that far away. Water sloshed into her mouth, stealing her voice.

The boat rose further from the water, until it towered over her, its rust shedding into the sea to reveal shell-work that glistened and covered every surface. The Shee bore the boat aloft, polishing the shells to iridescence, giant forms both in and of the sea.

The water of their bodies shifted and changed. They displayed their boat: this was the world they offered her. Something held her hair, keeping her head up and facing the boat. Music carried from it, the same song as at the portal yesterday. The music she'd danced to in the glen. It – the boat and the world it belonged to – could be hers. She moaned, and she didn't know if the sound betrayed fear or desire.

The boat surged forward with a roar. She touched it and knew it was real, not something she could dismiss. A shell flaked off and stuck to the back of her hand, a mark of intent.

Free yourself. She didn't know if it was the fairies' thought or her own. There was no distinction anymore. *No more fighting. No more deals.* Something brushed her ear. It pulled her hair back, leaned close. *Give us what we want.*

The sense of Simon came to her, his smell as she'd leaned against him last night – faint sweat, the freshness of the glen. She shook her head. "He isn't here," She'd kept him safe.

She reached for the boat, but it had pulled away. It had done what was needed – proved to her what the fairies were offering was real. The fingers twisted her in the water, passing her from one to the next, to the next, until she felt shingle under her feet and was able to stand, back at the inlet. The fairies opened a pathway through the passage. They shepherded her to the cavern where she'd parked the car, ushered her to the door and watched as she lifted the knife. Perhaps she could use it against them. The part of her held in thrall knew otherwise.

The air grew dank as she passed into the cave's depths. Dimmed sunbeams filtered through the gates blocking the other end. A sign caught the light and she squinted to read it:

Cave House. Private Residence and Grounds.

Someone lived beyond the gates. Hope flared in her: a

semblance of a chance to get away. She made out a driveway lined with rocks and lush green foliage, and tyre marks leading around the corner. They were recent, given the distinct imprint untouched by rain.

She tightened one hand around the black bars, willing someone to appear on the driveway and open the gate. The fairies flitted in and out between them, doing nothing to lift the loneliness that swamped her. The padlock fell loose, clattering to the ground. A sharp-eyed brownie grinned up at her.

The left gate swung open. Hands shoved Amy into the garden beyond. She skidded, fighting, her heels dug in. Loose stones gave no purchase, despite the tread on her stolen footwear. She rounded the corner of the driveway and gasped.

Fairies poured from every part of the garden alongside the driveway: from the trees, the grass, the flowers. The beat of their wings filled the air.

This wasn't a garden, it was a *nest*. She ran a short way onto the grass and sank to her knees, horrified. Her clothes hung heavy on her, the water dripping into the ground. Now she saw the shape of the trap.

She'd *told* Simon where she was going. Not in so many words, but in her description of the safety she craved. He'd work it out, sooner or later. She thought of the night before, slipping the acorn into his pocket as tears had streaked her face. The fairies had watched her do it. They had *let* her do it. They'd let her tell him about her safe place, let her give her talisman to him. There was no way he'd leave her exposed and scared. Despite their short time together, Amy had felt safe with him.

If he came, she'd run from him. She'd jump off the cliff

into the sea and take her chances before she'd hurt him.

A smell rose around her, the familiar dankness of old graves. She gagged against it, but it stayed strong, full of old knowledge. She couldn't stand against them here, not with so many. She wouldn't be able to phone for the help she'd planned. She pulled her knees to her chest. Hands stroked her back, her hair, touched her shoulders – no figment of her imagination – the tight feel of the petal against her skin, a soft burning confirmed it. And then the voices came again.

Chapter Twenty-Four

MARK FOLLOWED HIS dad to the crest of the hill and stopped to catch his breath. His mum joined them, map held open, tracing their path. She seemed more like herself, businesslike and focused on the search, with not a word about the fairies. Ever since she'd heard that Amy had been sighted, she'd been fine, and that reassured him. All the behaviour over the last day – the hardness, the distance – had been the result of nothing other than fear.

They'd long since left any decent tree cover. Heathland stretched in each direction, broken only by gorse bushes and the odd tree, bent and carved by the wind. Faerie-thorns. The sight of them made his stomach twist – tales he'd dismissed in Belfast took on a new menace here, in a land that left trees uncut for fear of the fairies and milk left on doorsteps to placate them.

"Amy!" Dad's voice echoed over the hilltop. He was above Mark, on a ridge of grey rock, his hands shading his eyes from the blazing sun. For an old boy he had stamina – the drink hadn't erased what years tending a boat had given him. "Amy, love, if you can hear me, come out."

Nothing but silence. Mark watched for any movement, disturbed birds, a flash of colour, but there was nothing. Nor could he see any signs of a deserted village. Not a ruin, or a house, or anything to suggest habitation.

He glanced at his mum, head down, lips moving as she scanned the map, and down at his watch. They'd been walking for at least twenty minutes, maybe more. These hills were easy to get turned around in. Unease settled, but he tried to ignore it. All they had to do was return to the church. He took another look around the barren hill. The path they'd followed vanished into stubby grass and bracken, with no sign of the church. His chest tightened.

"Mum," he said. His dad, perhaps picking up the worry in his voice, jumped down, landing with a soft thud beside Mark. "What did May say this morning? What did the farmer see?"

She looked up, her face composed and calm, almost angelic. "She said one of the local farmers was seeing to his flock, and he noticed Amy near the lost village."

Dad gave a soft curse. "Can you see anything missing from this picture?" He gestured all around.

She frowned. "Well, it's very remote. You'd hardly think it just a mile off the main road."

"Sheep." He glared at her. "Come on, Emma, whatever you are, you're not stupid. There are no sheep."

"You're right." She glanced at the map and then all around, her face innocent. "I'm sure we're in the right place. She did say he was moving the sheep."

Dad threw her a look that would have withered stone. "I don't know what game you're playing, Emma. But it needs to stop."

Nor did Mark. It made no sense for her to have lied about Amy being seen. They'd have been better staying near the house, searching the fields she had disappeared from yesterday. The police had moved on from there, after all, distracted by the report of the car theft. And if Simon had found her, the house was the first place he'd go to, surely. Unless his mother wanted him and his father off side. She knew they had been determined to search for Amy, perhaps she didn't want…

He glanced sharply at his mother, and put the thought out of his mind – she wanted Amy found, more than anyone. She'd been the constant in Amy's childhood, keeping her safe.

"No game at all." She waved the map. "I'm trying to do my best, just like you."

Dad took a step forward, then stopped, taking in the trails through the bracken, all of which led a few feet and then stopped. They were as likely to have been cast by the winds raking the hillside as people walking to the church or village.

Mark tried to quell the worry creeping through him, making his shoulders bunch and his breath catch. He tapped the map. "Which way?"

Mum pointed to her right. "Over the brow of the hill and down. We're just above the path. I'm not stupid. I know how to read a map."

He led the way, partially reassured. He forced his way through a stand of gorse bushes and went on for five minutes until he reached another clump of gorse blocking the path.

"This isn't the way," he said. "We didn't come through any gorse."

She chewed her lip, still calm – much calmer than Mark. "Oh, dear. Hold on until I get my bearings."

"Let me see." Dad took the map and stared at it. Mark craned to see. She had marked nothing and the OS map on its own was useless without a compass.

"Divining the way, were you?" asked Dad.

She snatched it back. "I was taking note of landmarks as we climbed. Mental notes, that is." She stared around. "I think we *are* in the wrong place."

Dad swore. His gaze jumped from furze to rock to tree, to Mark. "Any ideas?"

"Make sure we head down the hill?" The sea glittered like a shifting carpet of blue far below; if they walked towards the coast, they'd reach the main road at some point.

"We don't even know if we're on the right side of the fucking hill."

He was right. And it was miles away – it would take all day. Mark's hands made helpless fists. He forced himself to calm down. "It's better than nothing. Let's go."

They set off. He found himself walking beside Mum. Her gait was relaxed and loose-limbed. A small, knowing, smile danced on her lips.

All doubts left him: she *had* planned this. She didn't want them to find Amy. Even yesterday, she'd delayed as long as possible and fought against a proper search. He stopped, damned if he understood. Fear gripped him, making his blood chill. She had a history of psychosis; she could believe things that weren't real. He put his hand on her shoulder. He had to find out what she believed, one way or another. He turned her to face him.

CHAPTER TWENTY-FIVE

THE NORTHERN IRISH society of Sunday-drivers must have decided on Cushendun for a day out. Simon cursed as the taxi got stuck behind yet another car doing twenty. The twisting road offered no chance to pass, and the taxi man, on a meter, didn't seem inclined to anyway.

Simon checked the time on his phone and fought rising panic; it had taken him nearly half an hour to cover five miles, with the road getting busier all the time. If Amy had set off before the tourist traffic started she'd have a good head start. Enough that anything could have happened to her. He tried to divert himself but visions of her injured in the caves, or swept out to sea, wouldn't leave him.

That, or her being away with the – well, the usual word fit perfectly. What would he do then? It had been hard enough talking sense into her on the first night. What if she'd gone completely off the rails? He needed her family here, the people she trusted.

"Here, it'll be easier to walk from here." The taxi man pulled up in a lay-by before the bridge. "Thirty quid."

Jesus, they must be raking it in. Simon paid him, got out, and waited for the taxi to go, with a last glance in the mirror from the taxi driver.

He started down the road, passing the harbour at a jog. He turned the corner to the cave system and stopped, stunned. He'd expected a single small cave, not this line of looming rocks.

He stepped forwards, head craned back, scanning the cliffs. Trust Amy to have found somewhere as eerie as this. Why this should be her safe place was beyond him – it practically shouted spooky fairies.

The hairs on the back of his neck stood up, warning him not to go on, but he sped up, past jagged rocks which turned from grey to blood-red sandstone. The rocks stretched to his left, leading to sea. For someone like Amy, adept at hiding, it could be hours before he found her in this maze of rocks and sea and beach.

Waves reflected on the seaward rocks from a small cove on his left. His shoulders were tight, alert for any movement, but whilst there were plenty of signs of people – soft-drink bottles, crisp packets bleached by the sun, a discarded baby's dummy – the place was empty. On such a nice day, the beach had much more draw than the caves.

Either that, or something was keeping people from entering the caves. His breath stuttered, but he pushed the thought away. Amy believing in this fairy crap was bad enough, it wouldn't help if he did too.

Even so, he paused at the entrance to the single dark cave. It was easy to believe in something unexplained when facing places unchanged for years, full of legends and a sense of something different. No wonder Amy had succumbed yesterday.

Stale air replaced the brine. He hated the idea of going into that darkness, even though the passage was short enough to see sunlight at the other end. His fear was formless and made no sense – he had never been frightened of the dark. "Hello?" His shout echoed back.

He squared his shoulders. To hell with this; he had to find her. He stepped into the cave. The ground had a layer of dampness, allowing the impressions of tyres to reach into the shadows. The cave was just big enough for a car to be parked at an angle to the wall. Whoever the driver was, they hadn't passed the parallel parking module. Skin prickling, he approached it, keeping his footfalls soft, but it was vacant.

"Amy!" he called. He shivered, not just from the cold, but from the quiet stillness that surrounded him. He reached the barred exit from the cave. The gate was just ajar enough for someone to have slipped through. "Amy!" His voice cut through a steady beat of dripping water. Shining in the soft mud under the gate, a padlock lay open. Jesus, if the car was hers, Amy had been busy. Joy riding *and* breaking and entering. You had to hand it to the girl, she didn't do things by half.

Something moved in the small garden beyond, dashing behind a tall pampas grass. He darted forwards, down the long, narrow driveway that ran between two grassed lawns, ending in front of a three-storied house perched above the ocean. "Amy!?"

The garden was sultry and warm. Motes danced in the air around him, pollen or seed-heada, fogging the air. Another flash of movement made him jump.

For crying out loud, he wasn't some screaming girl in a horror flick, waiting for help. He was a six-foot-four rugby playing bloke, facing a girl who was sick, not some sort of monster.

"Amy!" The motes in the line of his breath moved and spun: everywhere else remained still and silent. His gaze jerked around, taking in the apple trees in the centre of the lawn to his left, the dog-roses clinging to the cliff to the right, framing the wilder end of the garden, full of long grass and brambles. She wasn't anywhere to be seen. The motes thickened, taking on a form of their own, shifting and circling around him. Behind, the gate closed with a crash.

INTERLUDE II

*T*HE LIGHT FROM *the candles on Amy's birthday cake reflected in her eyes. She smiled, glancing up through her dark hair, newly cropped. She didn't look like the fairy-girl I'd brought up. I sang along with the rest of the party, hardly daring to believe we'd made it to this day.*

Her dark eyes met mine. I could see the cunning in them. All the little signs I'd picked up over the years had been right. Her face had thinned, becoming heart-shaped and sharp: my daughter had been chubby and fat, not like Mark who'd been born thin and stayed thin. He was behind her, taking photographs as she blew the candles out. He lowered the camera and his eyes, dark and dashing, lacked the sly knowledge of hers. He had no idea what she was; Phil, propped against the door of the kitchen, shunned by most of the party, didn't know either. They were fools, pulled in by Amy's slyness.

My eyes fell on the candles circling the cake. Eighteen. She was an adult now. It was time. I'd kept her safe all these years, never allowing the fairies to take her back. I'd been there, throughout her childhood, bringing her home when she ran, making sure she kept the acorn with her, the talisman that had brought her back to me the first time, making sure she knew what she had to do when they called. Making sure she didn't leave with them too early. I'd been careful in other ways, too, nursing her through any sicknesses in a way I never nursed Mark, and fussing over her safety. I'd lost one fairy changeling; I knew the price I'd pay if I lost another.

Someone started three cheers and I joined in, feeling relaxed for the first time in years. Soon she'd go back to where she came from, and then my Amy would return. That's what the legends said; changelings were children living amongst us, not adults. She'd come back, and she'd be old enough and strong enough to bring Matty with her.

I bought the house in the glen, sure that the fairies would find Amy there. They did. From the first day, Amy saw them in the woods, in the shadows, in the lapping water on the beach. She sat by the river that ran behind the house, her lips moving as she sang, small songs I'd never heard in this world, and I saw, clearer than ever, how she wasn't the daughter I'd lost all those years ago, but a Not-Amy, a thing put in her place.

Not-Amy and her friends laughed at the idea the voices might be real, reducing their strength. It ate our food and enjoyed what life offered. It would never leave of its own accord; it needed to be encouraged.

And there was Mark. Always hovering, always bringing Not-Amy back when it took a step toward the otherworld. I watched him duped and made an idiot of. And Phil, with his erratic text messages and his little boat that Not-Amy had went to over the years and came back from, relaxed and calm. The filthy thing was taking over my daughter; it had stolen her childhood, it would never let her return. And without her, I'd never get Matty back. Matty, who I'd held in my arms, who'd cried, and then choked, and then went still. Stolen from me.

I bided my time and prepared. I told it about Matty, what he *looked like, his tufts of golden hair, from his father. I told it she'd bring him back to me one day. I talked, not knowing if my real daughter could hear me in her veiled world. If she did, she'd know that when she succumbed to the voices, she'd be free. That I'd take her back, no matter how long she'd been gone. I ached to hold her again and see her eyes without the aged knowledge they carried; watch her smile a real smile, not cunning and sure. I just had to give her the time to do what was needed.*

CHAPTER TWENTY-SIX

THE ROUGH BARK of the old apple tree ground against Amy's cheek. She rubbed her face up and down, seeking relief from the shooting pain in her head. She closed her eyes and tried to shut out the constant whispers, but the garden was too full of fairies, the noise from them too great.

She shivered in her still-damp clothes. She wanted someone with her, someone she could trust. Simon, if that had been possible: his lack of belief, his pragmatism, might put her back to the real world.

More than him, she wanted her dad. She wanted him to slick back her hair and tell her everything was all right. Typical; to want the one thing she couldn't have, the one person guaranteed not to come through for her.

Heat built from the sun, its rays wrapped in the sultry air. She opened her eyes and the light was green and unnatural. Somewhere, distantly, she knew she was sick, that the wound on her leg was hot and festering, but all she could do was tighten her arms around the trunk of the tree and hold on. It was either that or fall – and to fall here, in this nest…. She didn't think she'd ever get up again.

Her mother had promised that when it happened – when the fairies came – it would take time. She said they would have had to come a long way to reach Amy, all the way from fairyland, and it wouldn't be an easy journey to carry Amy back with them. But she hadn't said it would be a confused mess of sickness, a draining of her very self. She'd promised it would be pleasant, a last look at fairyland before Amy was too old, a chance to remember what it had been like as a child and to say goodbye.

She'd lied. The new knowledge twisted in Amy's guts, its significance ebbing and flowing, and she didn't know what it meant, only that if there was one lie there could be another.

Fairies drifted around her, coming in thicker and thicker droves: a prelude to something unknown. A wash of ice broke through her fever, a panic that seized her heart and tightened. But they didn't come close. There were no hands on her shoulders, no tinkled laughter in her ear. They were waiting, sure and knowing in the way only old creatures could be.

A brief flash in the side of her vision reminded her what they were waiting for. Her right hand, clutching the knife, tightened. It sickened her, knowing why she had it.

Perhaps she could go down to the house. Hand over the knife and ask for a doctor. She tried to straighten her legs to take her own weight, but they would barely hold her up, let alone carry her to the end of the long lawn and over the courtyard.

The walls started to imprint onto her eyes and her headache grew worse. The house came and went, sharp then dull, until it became a grey blur in the distance and nothing more.

She sank to the ground and sat, leaning against the tree. She set the knife on the grass beside her, her fingertips brushing the blade. The cliffs surrounding the garden muffled any sounds except the drone of bees and the chirrup of crickets. On another day it would have been pleasant.

Metal scraped against rock, shocking her. She shook her head, groggy from the heat. The garden's scent had changed from soft florals to a heavier, earthy smell. A chill cut through the Indian-summer day, as if a shadow had fallen over her – yet still the sun drummed down.

The waiting fairies stopped drifting. Their faces grew pinched, their eyes flashing. A clang echoed through the air and she knew what the metal rasp had been. Someone was coming into the garden.

She squinted, heart pounding, and watched the path to the gate. She couldn't hear the thrum of an engine or the coarse sound of tyres on the driveway threshold; the visitor was on foot.

A moment later, Simon emerged from behind the path's foliage. She blinked, willing herself to be wrong. Not in this den, so close and hot, with so many voices around her. When she looked again, he was still there. Golden sun streamed through his hair and made him look like a Greek hero, all sun-burnished and solid.

The fairies had been right about him coming. That meant they must be real. A sick metallic taste flooded her mouth at the realisation of what, and who, she was.

On balance, she'd prefer to be mad. There was hope in a mental condition: hope that it could be cured; that she might ride the episode out as she had every other time. But against this? She'd be lost.

Worse – she'd be *glad* to be lost. They'd make her want to stay, using their glamour nectar-coated poison, and all the while she'd know, somewhere deep inside, that she'd been Amy who'd enjoyed real sunshine, the taste of the spray hitting her lips on her dad's boat. She'd know that she'd once been held and kept safe.

Her right hand twitched. It clasped the knife. She looked down to see two pixies, the size of her hand, solid muscles cording their arms. They forced her fingers around the hilt until her knuckles were white.

She tried to loosen her fingers, narrowing her eyes in focus. She imagined her knuckles unfolding and the hilt peeling from her palm.

Nothing. Her fingers stayed tight. Simon came further up the path, looking all around. In a moment, he'd be past the grasses lining the pathway and he'd see her for sure.

The faces surrounding her – in the trees, on the grass, in the sky – took on the shape of the fairy at the B&B, the one who'd urged her to hurt Simon. The teenagers had gone, morphed into something cunning and sly.

"I don't want to," she tried to say, but it came out as nothing more than a croak. She licked her lips. They were dry and cracked from the saltwater earlier. "Why must I?"

But she already knew the answer to her crumpled question. She had to let go of her future in this world.

"But he's not my future." Didn't they know that? Simon was a bloke she'd met who'd been nice to her. Whatever they'd shared last night, deep in the glens, would be gone when they returned to Belfast and their separate lives. No other bloke had been able to cope with the reality of her madness; why would he be any different? There was no need to hurt him.

No, the fairies insisted, they knew, she had to trust them. To be with them she had to leave her future behind, and he *was* her future. Images flickered of her on another day, in a world with no voices, wearing a wedding dress. Simon stood beside her, in a suit with a flower on its lapel, his eyes drinking her in. She lifted her hand, trying to reach him.

"Amy!" His voice pulled her back to the garden. He strode over the grass, covering the ground quickly. Dread grew in her.

The fairies circled her, protective – or possessive. She dug the nails of her free hand into the bark of the tree, so deep they ripped to the quick. She welcomed the pain – it might hold her to what was real.

It didn't work. She got to her feet, her movements slow and unsteady, helped by the hands of the fairies who forced her upright, head lolling to the side. Simon approached, eyes wary. What had he seen to make him so unsure?

"Amy," he said, relief heavy in his voice. She tried to warn him to stay back, but her throat was too thick, as if she'd swallowed something.

Her head came up. Alertness flooded her, a wave of injected adrenaline. The knife's solid hilt dug into her palm. The fairies had waited fourteen years. They wouldn't wait any longer. She brought the knife up.

Chapter Twenty-Seven

D AD JOINED MARK on the hillside. He sucked in a breath, and then another, slow and measured. Tight muscles showed under his thin, tanned skin. He'd never been angrier, Mark realised.

"You don't *want* her to be found?" His voice was husked and low; he seemed on the verge of reaching out and shaking Mum but she didn't flinch away. Instead, her eyes flashed, matching his, but with something that wasn't anger. Belief, maybe, or a sense of pride.

Mark knew the look well, from the nights his mother had sat with Amy, telling her she was special and should listen to the voices. He knew it from the day he'd been ordered to leave. Amy had been screaming that she couldn't do this, that she was nuts, but his mum had given him a cold glare that told him she'd won. Once again, on this hillside, she'd forced them all into *her* decision, not caring that no one else would agree. Anger built, radiating through his veins, making him feel alive. *This* was what he sought, in the depths of a kicking – the sense he was human and real. She smiled, and his anger grew. She'd played them all for fools.

"Oh, Phil," she said. "Of course I want her found. Just not yet."

"Why not?" demanded Mark. "She needs us."

She dismissed the question with a toss of her head, the way she'd dismissed him in preference for Amy. Amy, who needed help and was special; Amy, who was sick; Amy, who wanted none of the attention but still got it.

It felt good to be angry. Good to feel *something*. She was his mum, after all, who'd come to his sport-days and cheered even when he'd crossed the finish line last; who'd sent him out for his first job in a suit she'd pawned a necklace to buy. Surely, somewhere, that mother must still exist.

He planted his feet. "Why, Mum?"

She gave a smile. This wasn't the knowing smile of earlier, or the sly one of the wedding disco, but something soulless. It chilled him. She knew he'd do nothing to her, that he wasn't capable of hurting her. She held him as firmly as when he was a child who'd known it was his fault Amy had been lost, that he should have watched for her in the little glen.

He glanced at his father. He'd been looking after Amy, too, that day. He'd been the adult and still hadn't been able to stop it happen. Amy, even then, could never be held on to. He wanted to tell his younger self, running up the site, fear chasing him, that he had caused nothing, and could stop even less.

"Now she's an adult, it's time," said his mum. A maddening edge tinged her voice, a flatness that defied any rebuttal. "We'll get her back. Matty, too."

Matty, the baby she lost. The baby she'd once believed

had been taken.

"Matty?" His dad looked stunned. "Matty's dead."

"He's not." She was matter of fact, as if they should know. "The changeling died, not Matty." She smiled, and it looked almost sane. "You must have known Amy was changed. Now she's an adult, they'll take *their* Amy back, and when *ours* returns, she'll bring Matty with her."

Mark's throat tightened, his eyes moist. How could his mother have got so lost in this fantasy? Fear came with the sadness. If she really believed this, she was sick. Sicker than Amy. The roots of everything he'd known seemed to shrivel, a changed landscape he didn't know how to fight.

"Oh, Jesus Christ." His dad grabbed her arm. "Emma, this is nuts. You must know it. Amy is out there, alone, and we don't have time to be walking in circles."

"They won't hurt her. She's one of them." Mum pulled free and started to pace, trailing footmarks through the stubbed grass. "Her eyes," she said, her voice calm and certain. She stabbed at her own, making Mark wince. "Haven't you noticed? They're dark."

"So are Mark's." Dad pushed him in front of her. "Look."

She kept pacing, her shoulders straight and determined. She circled him and Mark, trapping them.

"They're not the same." Her words were coming quicker. "Hers are like pools. They hide things. Neither of you could ever see the truth. You would have had to face what you'd done." She was close to raving.

Dad shook his head. "Amy's sick. No one did anything to her."

"Liar." She laughed, but it wasn't a real laugh. "The fairies took her and left a monster in her place."

Mark met his dad's shocked eyes. This wasn't a one-off thought, brought about by the strain of Amy getting lost again. It wasn't a voice that could be dismissed and forgotten. This was belief in something that simply could not be. He'd been around Amy's doctors for long enough to know there was no easy fix for something like this. There'd be doctor after doctor, and her fighting all the way.

"Mum," he said. He reached for her hand. He had to find a way to connect with her and make her see sense, despite what she had done to him. She didn't let him take her hand, twisting away at his touch, as if it burned her. Still, he held his hand out to her. "Think about what you're saying. It's not possible."

"It's true. She's a changeling." No looking away, no questioning edge, just a statement of fact.

"Enough," Dad said. "Try the police, Mark, and see if we can get an update." Mark tried his phone, but got only the dead signal. He flicked the handset off, preserving what little charge was left. "Nothing."

"Fuck."

Mark started down the hill, following trails that petered into nothing. Two or three of them were wider, as if they might become something useful, but they led in different directions. He turned to his parents, above him on the hill. "We have to get back."

"Fine." Mum opened her arms. "Lead the way. By the time you work out a way down, it'll be too late. They'll have taken her. She's been away two days; she must be with them. I'll have my Amy back where she should have been all along. Where *you* let her escape from."

His dad grabbed her wrists, holding them tight, and Mark could see that his anger wasn't even close to being held back. He'd had years of trying to deal with this, Mark remembered, years of being batted away and denied. His father leaned his face close to hers. She flinched.

"We're getting off this mountain." Every word was firm and clear. "We're going to find Amy. And then I'll deal with you." He dropped her arms. "Right, which way?"

Mark scanned the hill, his heart sinking. His mother was right. Amy would be far into her own world, and this time he hadn't been there to pull her back. It was all a bloody mess, one that they should have seen coming, or been able to read. Except – there'd been no hints that something like this had gripped his mother. She'd been too clever, or too fixed in her belief that she was doing the right thing, for any of them to know.

Like the child he'd been, logic didn't stop his guilt. Once again, he'd have to live with the knowledge that he'd let Amy down. If she didn't come back, he didn't know how he could.

Chapter Twenty-Eight

S IMON HURRIED OVER to Amy, eyes never leaving her. He'd been so sure, when he'd looked down the driveway at the house perched over the sea, that she'd have gone over the cliff. Only now did he realise the fear that had been coursing through him from the moment he found the acorn.

"Amy," he called. "Thank God you're here." She didn't respond but stood, watching. She didn't look steady on her feet, and her face was flushed, her eyes glassy. He slowed a little; he didn't want to frighten her into running, and if she was as sick as she looked, she'd be easily confused.

"Amy, you're not in any trouble." He winced at that lie. Once the police arrived, she had a lot of explaining to do. "Will you come with me, and I'll get Mark for you?"

Nothing but stretching silence and the sun's heat, beyond anything that should be possible in Northern Ireland by the coast, where sea breezes kept even blistering days cool.

The smell of the garden, soil still damp from the rain of

the previous evening, came in deep waves of flowers and loam. It made him light-headed: the heat, the smell, his worry. Amy didn't move; didn't say anything. She just watched him, her big eyes pleading for something he didn't understand. Her hand held something half-hidden by her skirt.

Pollen motes thickened around him, so dense he could see them. He waved his hand in front of his face and felt them on his skin, pitting and fizzing like living creatures. He took another step forward, letting them encircle him.

"Amy, come over. I'm here to help."

HE WAS HERE *to help*. She watched, mouth unmoving, as he walked across the grass. Couldn't he see the fairies all around him? Or feel the one sitting on his shoulder, its face turned to him, so close he should be able to feel its breath on his neck and hear the beat of its wings? He waved his hand in front of him, as if he had noticed the horde, and she leaned forward, ready for him to realise it wasn't voices in her head. Ready for him to realise she'd been right, and that he was in danger. *Run*, she willed him. *Go back, through the caves, and never return.*

Her hand clenched around the knife. Fairies streamed from everywhere, flitting between Simon and herself, making sure she knew what to do. More stayed on the tree, surrounding her. Guarding her.

Her breathing was quiet and halting. She wanted this moment to stop, and for Simon to leave the garden with his future ahead of him. She'd sacrifice herself, if he could just stay alive. *Run*. Her lips moved; no sound came out.

Simon's face crinkled with worry. The fairy on his shoulder turned its head to Amy and bared its teeth.

Make it quick for him. If you leave him to us, it won't be. Fairies circled her. *Won't be, won't be, won't be.*

The smell of the garden rose around her, putrid and old, making her gag against it. A shadow reached across the grass to her, fingers searching. It touched her ankle, pinning her in place, the long bone of its joint cold and sharp. Her head went back, a scream stopped in her throat by another set of fingers, just as cold. She could feel the power in its touch, power enhanced by the dog's death, and suddenly she knew.

Simon was a sacrifice for her to leave one life for the next. There was no ancient portal here, linking the worlds – the Earth needed more than she could give. His blood for her release, the Earth drinking him in, adding to its ancient power. She could see it clearly, how his blood would leak through the soil, bringing the two worlds together, enriched by what he could have been to her. If the dog's death had given the shadows so much power, how much more would Simon's?

The fingers held her, letting the knowledge sink in. Her throat was pinched closed, stopped of any words.

Simon paused by a grass-like plant with long strands of purple flowers dancing, like puppets on a string. She stayed against the tree, as silent as the garden itself. With her free hand she rubbed the tree-trunk behind her, focusing on the rough bark, real under her skin in a way the shadow fingers could never be. She closed her eyes and tried to remember the world she'd grown up in, the house before the one in the woods. Her room had looked out over a garden filled with scooters and bikes and a little play-house that she'd loved and Mark had hated. That was the real world, the one she should cling to. She remembered being with Tori. They used to laugh so much at everything. She tried to hold those memories, but they faded until only this loamy garden filled her senses.

Now, now, now…

The fairies could taste her weakness. Simon crossed the lawn towards her, his arms by his side, muscles tight with tension. Could he sense the danger surrounding him?

Another fairy landed on his shoulder. It laid its mouth, with its twisted, sharp teeth against his throat. *If you don't take him, we will.* It stretched long fingers over his shoulder and towards his chest. *We'll eat out his heart.* He reached his hand to his neck. If he could feel the fairy, they *could* hurt him. Its mouth stretched open, ready to bite.

"No!" She ripped the scream past the fingers, pulling herself to the side. The shadow tore away. She *couldn't* let them have him.

"Amy." Simon's face was masked with worry and relief, but his eyes met hers, unflinching. "I'm here. You're all right now."

She shook her head. She raised the knife. "You came," she said. "You shouldn't have."

"AMY." THE COLOUR of her dress, the soft greens and pinks, merged with the garden. Her shoes, some sort of garish trainers, glittered in the sun. On anyone else they'd have looked ridiculous, childish even, but she made them look good. "I'm here. You're all right now."

Gashes covered her arms and legs, worse than before. The particularly nasty one on her leg oozed dark blood, the skin around it red and swollen. She was thinner, her face pinched, both the Amy from yesterday and a changed one. He took a step towards her. "I'm here. You're all right now."

Her eyes were deep pools of exhaustion. Two days: she'd been fighting her demons for two days.

She raised her right hand and the sun glistened off a long blade. He stared at the knife, not quite believing it was real, but as she lifted it higher, he could see the thin blade and her tight hand around it. *Jesus.* His chest tightened and his muscles bunched, ready to fight or run. She twisted the knife and he saw its sharpness and slender menace. She didn't smile, or look away, just held his gaze.

"You came," she said, her words croaked and dry. She was swaying on her feet, barely strong enough to stand let alone wield a knife. She didn't look angry or dangerous. She just looked scared. "You shouldn't have."

He lifted the acorn from his pocket, holding it out between two fingers, like the talisman it was to her. He drew himself straight, fighting the urge to run, readying to move the moment she did. Even with the knife, he should be able to stop her, sick as she was.

"You don't have to do this," he said, and held the acorn out. She followed his movements, not looking once at the knife in her hand. He couldn't even tell if she knew she had it. "Take your acorn back, and we'll find a way of keeping you safe." He took a cautious step forwards. "We were worried," he said. Keep her talking, he remembered. The night at the waterfall, talking had been what kept her with him, even if everything he'd said had been utter shite. He tried to smile, and knew it must look like a grimace. "Your parents and Mark, they're looking for you…"

"My parents?" Her free hand clutched the tree beside her. If she passed out, it would be perfect; he'd get the knife off her and take things from there quite happily. She straightened a little. *Damn.*

"Mark called them," he said.

She licked her lips. "My dad came?"

"Yeah." He didn't known if he had, May hadn't said, but he saw the naked need in her eyes. To hell with not lying; right now he'd say anything he needed to get her to safety. "He's looking for you. He'll be glad to see you." He held out his hands, one empty and open, the other holding the acorn. "Give me the knife and we'll call him."

She shook her head. "I can't." The blade waved a little. She let go of the tree and put her other hand on the hilt. A tendril of hair had stuck to her cheek. He wanted to reach out and push it away for her. Her neck shone with sweat.

"Amy, you're not well." He reached to within inches of the knife. Let him get through to her. "Please, let's get you out of here and back to your family. I can make it all right if you'll just let me help."

She followed the movement of his hand, swishing him away with the knife. "You have to go."

"Go?" He held his hands out. *Don't scare her.* "Yeah, I think we should. Come on. You can tell me about how you got a car." She didn't answer. Her eyes looked past him, into the air. He looked around, and then back. There was nothing there except Amy, and the knife glistening in the sun.

Her hand twitched. She took a step forward. Her eyes darted from him to the garden and back to him in a trapped circle. He stayed where he was. She wouldn't use the knife. He knew she wouldn't, not the Amy from yesterday, who'd laughed when he'd called her a fairy-hunter. A part of him was astounded at his calmness; another yelled at him to get away from her. He held out his hand. "Give it up and we'll go."

"Run." Her voice was thin and forced, her eyes beseeching. A shadow crossed the ground between them, long and thin. Her mouth was in a thin line, as if fighting for the words. She leaned towards him, and said through clenched teeth, "Simon, run."

HE DIDN'T MOVE. She'd told him to run, pulling the words from the very core of her, and he didn't understand. He just waited, hands out. Her acorn shone in his fingers and she wanted to take it, but the fairies wouldn't allow her; they knew her belief in it was as strong as her belief in them.

Do it now! Kill him! The fairies were stronger, rending their will on her, but she fought them, holding the knife with both hands. She couldn't hold firm much longer. Her hands shook; it was hard to keep fighting.

The fairies surrounding him all had old faces. The teenage gaggle weren't coming back, it seemed.

"You need to get out," she said. He had to be made to understand. "They're going to hurt you."

"Amy." His eyes were pleading. "Please, Amy, listen to me. Don't listen to them; they're not real."

Anger filled the garden, darting shapes of hissing hatred. The shadow crossed his feet, started up his legs. They'd eat his heart out, they'd said.

She shook her head, but it was no good; she was a stranger she'd never wanted to be, one who thought things that were alien to her. Her hand moved but it wasn't her doing it. It wasn't her who knew exactly where to put the blade to hurt him. *Kill him.*

She lunged forward. He brought his hand up, deflecting the knife, and let out a yell. A long line of red beaded along his palm. She pulled the knife back.

"Go!" she said. "They're going to make me do it."

He stumbled back. The fairies surged at him, and it was too late for him to run. His face drained of colour. The fairies on his shoulder stood, ready to guide her hands. He staggered back two steps, until blocked by a willow tree.

The fairies urged her on, voice upon voice. Thin fronds descended from the tree, wreathing Simon. One circled his neck, flittering in the sun, holding his chin back, exposing his throat. He lifted his hand to pull it away, but the frond didn't give. His eyes widened; he knew what was happening. At last, he knew. He pulled harder at the frond, highlighting its green with sharp red blood from his hand.

Now. Her steps guided themselves. She raised the knife, heart thudding. His wrists were taken, held by the fairies and wrapped in the withies. He struggled to free himself. *Helpless Simon, tell them they're not real now if you can.* He shook his head; mouthed 'Amy', but Amy wasn't here, just something wearing her ruined body. The shadow halted, near his heart – either she did this, or it did. She brought the knife down with all her strength.

"Don't listen!" His words cut the air, reaching something deep inside her.

She wrenched the knife to the side, so it trailed along his skin instead of stabbing into his neck. He screamed and wrenched clear. He fell to the ground, left hand over his right shoulder. Blood trickled through his fingers and down the back of his hand. His eyes met hers, pleading.

Finish it: a cacophony of words, denting her knowledge of herself. She pushed her hair back from her forehead; it was soaked through with sweat. Her hand burned when she touched her skin.

"Don't listen." Simon's voice sounded thin, nothing like it had been. Blood trickled down his arm, forming into rivulets. With what seemed like huge effort he brought his head up and looked directly at her. "You don't have to."

She knelt by him and touched his lips. They were soft and dry. He moved them against her finger, a kiss or a word, she didn't know.

"I'm sorry," she whispered. Her other hand was moving, lifting without guidance. She tried to open the fingers, to drop the knife, but they were held tight against it.

Simon's breathing was ragged. His eyes, pain-filled, didn't look away from hers. In the grass beside him the acorn shone, its gold smeared with the red of his blood. "Don't answer them; just go."

She dropped her finger from his lips. His gaze followed and supported her. She lifted her chin. "I won't do it." Her words were directed into the air and through the garden. "You can't make me." She scrabbled for the acorn, dirt sticking under her nails as she snatched it up.

The fairies' screams drowned out the sound of the sea. Amy forced her hand open and dropped the knife. She got to her feet, the acorn held against her. She could not be trusted. She could not trust herself. She took a last look at Simon before turning away. She knew, now, the truth: she had to go back to the boat.

CHAPTER TWENTY-NINE

MARK POINTED TO a rivulet of water, one which had been joined by others and was redefining itself as a stream. "Follow it?" he suggested. It had to be as good a plan as any other. "It has to take us out somewhere."

His dad nodded and they set off, staying close to the stream. He kept hold of one of his mum's arms, but she wasn't fighting, but nor was she cold like earlier. Instead, she had a small smile on her face, serene and calm. She was muttering under her breath, the same words over and over – a poem, he thought. She appeared oblivious to either of the men, as if her explanations on the hillside had solved things. Now it wasn't just her burden, it seemed – and, without her self-appointed guardianship of Amy's future and past, she appeared lost. It was impossible to be angry with her, not when she was so broken.

"You're right," said Dad, as the furzed grass thinned and become a path tracking the water. "This has to come out somewhere."

The sea glistened below: closer, Mark was sure of it.

They hurried. Mum kept going with her poetry recital, on and on about the waters and the wild. He vaguely recognised it from school: something by Yeats. He frowned, remembering some of the detail – about changelings calling human children into the wild. Fear gripped him, threatening to paralyse him, here on this hillside where time moved too quickly, fairies and changelings felt too real. He tightened his grip on her arm. "Come on, Mum, let's get to the car."

She smiled at him, maddeningly calm, but her eyes shone with zeal. She'd won. She knew it, and in his heart he did, too. There was no way Amy could have lasted this long and not be very, very ill. His throat tightened, and breathing was hard. Very, very ill was the best-case scenario.

The sound of voices cut into his thoughts. He stopped. "Shhh."

Dad nodded. "Below us."

"I'll go," he said. Anything would be preferable to listening to her any longer. "You stay with Mum."

He didn't give his dad a chance to argue, but took off, half-running, half-skidding down the trail. He turned a corner and almost ran into a group of ramblers making their way up the hill. They looked professional, reflectors on their backpacks and good, thick walking boots. He sent a silent prayer of thanks. The ramblers stopped at his clattering steps.

"Can you help me?" Mark gasped. He needed to start going to the gym again. He leaned forward and put his hands on his knees.

"Take your time, get your breath back."

Mark nodded up at a thick-set man who handed him a water bottle. He straightened and took a long drink, only realising how thirsty he'd been when it slaked his dry throat.

He wiped his mouth and handed the bottle back.

"Thanks. We left our car at Ardclinnis Church a couple of hours ago. We came off the trail and got turned around, and we need to get back. It's very urgent."

"Ardclinnis?" One of the younger walkers leaned over a map. She, at least, had a compass with her and didn't seem to be relying on landmarks. Mark's hand tightened into a fist; how could he have been so stupid? He'd *known* Mum was up to something. He swallowed; there'd be time for a post-mortem later. He winced at his thought. Please, God – don't let a postmortem be needed.

"That's about three miles away, mate. Over the hill." The walker frowned. "You'd be quicker going down to the village and calling a taxi."

Brilliant; hours in the hills to get back where they started from. "So, we just follow the stream?"

The rambler nodded. "About half a mile, mate."

His parents arrived, a little out of breath, and Dad nodded at the ramblers. His mum paid them no heed, but went on mumbling her poem.

The older rambler's face creased into a frown. "Is she okay?"

"Yeah." How did he explain? *Don't mind my mother, she's just lost her marbles and sacrificed my sister to God-knows-what.* Something of the fear burning in him must have shown, because the rambler's face grew more concerned.

Dad leaned close to the rambler, and said, in a low voice, "She's communing with nature." He pointed to his head and mimed a circle, and Mark had to bite back a laugh he'd never imagined making in the circumstances. *That*, at least, was accurate.

"One of *them*." The rambler nodded sagely. "Well, each

to their own."

The group left and Mark blew out a breath. "Right. Let's go." They followed the river. The going got easier, until they could see the village below. Mark glanced at his mum. She might be nuts, but she'd been bloody effective.

Chapter Thirty

S IMON LAY, TEETH gritted, his face against the soft grass. Three years of semi-pro rugby and he'd never felt pain like this, stabbing right through his muscle, sending sick spasms up and down his arm. Blood oozed steadily from his shoulder, darkening the grass.

The image of Amy just before she had stabbed him replayed. Her eyes had been round and wild, not fey but deadly. Her slenderness had seemed a weapon of stealth, of speed. He still – on the fourth replay of it, each one in horrendous, sharp detail – couldn't quite believe she'd stabbed him.

His shoulder twitched, sending fresh pain. She'd done it all right, and it wouldn't help if he bled out on the lawn. He forced himself to move, biting back a yell as his muscles bunched. He got to his knees and sat, waiting for the pain to ebb. A wave of dizzy nausea convinced him not to try to stand just yet. He clamped his right hand, with its matching cut, on his shoulder to slow the bleeding.

He waited for the dizziness to pass. The image of the

knife flashed again: the quick speed, the sudden pain. He flinched. The flashback started again. Slower this time, so slow he should have been able to push her away before she stabbed him.

His neck; the knife had been aimed at his neck. He craned his head to look at his shoulder, hissing at the movement. The wound wasn't as bad as he'd feared, more a jagged, shallow, gash than the gaping horror he'd expected. It hurt like hell, yes, but his muscle hadn't been cut into, or any bone exposed. But if it had been his neck....

He closed his eyes and replayed the attack again. He focused on Amy's face. It had been twisted, as if fighting something. The knife flashed and he saw how it slid from the downward motion and lost something of its strength.

She'd said she was sorry and held her finger against his lips. She'd forced the knife from its deadly path. The violence hadn't come from *her* – the real Amy he'd chatted to in the B&B, who was able to take a joke about the fairies, and talk about a life he could never stand in a matter-of-fact fashion.

Calmer, he replayed the scene, taking it past the arc of the knife. She'd snatched something from the grass before she'd run and he knew what it must have been. His mouth stretched into a smile.

"You aren't having her, you fuckers," he said, loud enough to carry through the garden, to disperse into the pollen clouds, to reach the cliff and up it. If there was anything listening, let them know he wasn't scared. Even if he was. "She deserves better."

He staggered to his feet. Brave words aside, he had to find Amy. She'd been driven to take a knife to him; who knew where the voices might take her next. He thought of the path to the caves, the harbour at the mouth of the cove, the beach at the other side of it, full of kids and not five minutes away. Panic threatened, bubbling up from his stomach. He gritted his teeth, put his hand on the wound, and stumbled across the grass to the driveway.

The gate to the caves lay open, as if inviting him into the darkness. He stepped in, glaring all around. The worst thing about Amy's imaginings was that he didn't know what she could see, and what needed to be fought. The sound of the sea echoed, a hollow swish of incoming waves, the low drag of the surf pulling out. He reached the cove he'd passed coming in, the narrow shingle beach that led to the vast sea beyond. A cramp wrenched his shoulder, but he ignored it. Turning into the cove, balancing precariously the cobbles, he made his way towards the sea. He needed to be methodical in searching for her – he couldn't afford her to get behind him.

The rock walls hemmed him in, trapping him. He stumbled onto the narrow shingle beach, water sucking the shingle between his toes. Seagulls keened from above; it sounded like screams. He stepped forward, to the edge of the water, looking over the horizon, hardly aware that his lips were moving in a barely remembered prayer.

DAD BUNDLED MUM into the back seat of the taxi, half-guiding, half-pushing her, and followed her in. Mark clambered in the other side, so she was between them.

"Old Ardclinnis church," he said. He took out his phone and quickly checked it. Mercifully, a text had come through on the sputtering one-bar of signal, and he thumbed it open.

Be the police. Say Amy had been found and was well. He read the text, and his mouth fell open.

"Change of plan," he said. "That was from Simon. He says he thinks he knows where she's gone."

"Is she okay?"

He'd said nothing about how she was. "I don't know." He swallowed the familiar acid-rush of worry, and leaned forward to tap the driver's shoulder. "We need to get to Cushendun. Quickly."

"This isn't Police, Camera, Action," snarked the driver, but he turned the car in a tight sweep at the end of a country road, and headed up the coast road.

"Cheers." Mark tried the number on the text message, but it cut off. He tapped the phone against his leg as if that might make it work better.

The caves at Cushendun. He remembered sailing to them, helping his dad on the boat. It had taken all three of them to bring the boat in through the treacherous stretch of coastline, full of twisting currents and hidden rocks. The sea was the North Atlantic, all the way from America. Even on a hot day, it would be freezing.

His dad tapped his fingers in rhythm with Mark's phone. His jaw was set tight. He knew, even better than Mark, what the sea could do. He also knew how Amy might react to the coast if she was sick. He'd held her on the pontoon as she'd described creatures in Strangford Lough, creatures that she could see and talk to. Mark had sat close, soaked t-shirt pooling beside him, breathing heavy from the rescue of her, and listened as Dad had got her to her feet and taken her to the end of the pontoon.

He'd pointed over the sound's fast waters, showing her how the seals made shapes in the water, how they could make it appear moving and alive.

She'd insisted the Shee were still there, calling her. She'd tried to break away and go back in and Mark had tensed, but his dad had stopped her, encasing her in his strong arms.

In the end, desperate, Dad had given her some of his Librium, left over from his last attempt at detoxing. As soon as she was malleable enough, he'd taken her back to Belfast. And the whole way, all the way up the winding peninsula road and through the city, she'd cried and asked him to promise to take her back to the lough. The Shee were waiting, she'd said. The Shee who weren't like the other fairies, who were older, more knowledgeable.

"Mark," said his dad. "Call the police. Tell them to get to her."

He was right. Whatever trouble Amy was in, they could deal with later. He made the call, quickly, and left a message, his phone cutting off just as he finished. He stared at the handset – he had to hope it had been enough and the message would get through to the people who needed to hear it.

"It'll be all right," he said. His dad gave a wavering smile, which did nothing to fool either of them. Mark turned away, not able to face the sad eyes, and the fear that filled them. Or his mother's little smile and constant murmurs. He focused on the ocean and tried to think of something – anything – other than Amy wading in, deeper and deeper, until her dress was lifted by the current and she was taken.

SIMON LET OUT his breath, not aware he'd been holding it. Amy stood off to one side, at the very edge of the surf, her back turned to him. She showed no sign of hearing his approach as he picked his way over, careful not to startle. He dropped his good hand from his shoulder – the bleeding had slowed to a trickle and the pain had settled to a dull ache. He'd been lucky; the gash wasn't as deep as it could have been.

"Amy," he said. He kept his voice low, and kept his distance. There was no guarantee he'd keep being lucky. "Can you hear me?"

She turned to him, her face flushed. Her gaze jumped from him to the rocks behind, to the sky, and back to him. Her lips were bleeding from her biting down on them. He stopped a few feet in front of her, his shoulder against the cliff wall.

"I'm sorry." Amy's voice was halting and faint. "I couldn't stop them."

"Shhh. It's all right."

"It's not." He had to strain to hear her. "They're waiting for me."

It wasn't over. The hope left him, mimicking his shoes sinking into the shingle as if life was being sucked from him. She hadn't run far enough.

"Amy…" He didn't know what to say to reach her. He moved so that he was beside her.

Her eyes were fixed on the sea. The murderous look was gone; she looked more like the girl he'd first met at the waterfall than the frenzied girl in the garden. She swayed in rhythm with the waves, lifted her hand and pointed. "Can you see it?"

"What?" he asked. The sea was empty of anything but

endless lines of white surf, breaking and running to shore, one after the other.

"There's a boat," she said. "But it's not of this world." She gave a small smile, as if embarrassed. "It wants me. Then it will go."

He squinted. There was nothing. "Amy…" He shook his head, completely out of his depth. "There's nothing there." He leaned against the rock cliff. "You don't look well and I need a doctor. Please, Amy."

"Don't. You can't come near me. I can't be trusted." She backed away. "Don't follow me. It's not safe for you." She turned, jewelled shoes flashing as she raced surefooted across the beach, more goat than girl. He grabbed for her, but she was too quick.

"Amy!" He stumbled after her. His ankle caught between two rocks and wrenched. He yelled, but he kept going, half-hopping. He'd once managed half a rugby match with his ankle cold-frozen to keep him on his feet, he was damned if he was going to stop now.

Amy reached the edge of the sea and started to wade into it.

"Amy! Stop. There's nothing there!"

She was already in the water up to her thighs. A wave pulled her off balance, but she righted herself. She half-dived, submerging all but her head, and started to dog-paddle.

Simon reached the water's edge. He pulled off his shoes, adrenalin masking any pain, and then his trousers. The water gurgled and sucked around the base of the rocks. He checked for Amy – treading water, sheltered in the natural harbour of the cove for now. If she went much further out, she'd hit the open sea, with waves crashing every minute.

He looked at the rocks to the side of the arch. The current there was vicious, its twisting tides dashing the waves against the rocks.

She began to make her way towards the rocks, eyes focused on a patch of water just before them. *Shit*. There was no time to call the police, no hope of the coastguard reaching this small cove in time.

He dived forwards, yelling as he pulled his arm up, and thrust himself into the surf. The water hit his face, salt stinging, cold forcing the breath from his lungs. He'd be lucky if he didn't have a heart attack. He spat water and swam forwards. "Amy!"

Where was she? He trod water, searching for her, but he'd got turned around and lost his bearings. Seaweed wound around his legs, slick fingers of an obscene lover. He turned in a circle, so he was facing the caves.

Amy bobbed a few feet to his right, face serene. There was, he confirmed, no boat, of this world or any other.

Chapter Thirty-One

A MY KICKED HER legs and pushed through the current with her arms. Now she was in, the water wasn't as cold; at the start it had been like a knife cutting to the centre of her.

The boat loomed over her, its shell sides glistening. *Her* boat. Once she reached it, everything would be over. No more fighting. No more questioning, just acceptance that things could go on no longer.

She'd hurt Simon for the fairies. Not just him: over the years, she'd hurt her parents and Mark. All the nights of worry, of sitting up with her. There was no place for her in this world, not if the fey-world would keep coming back to her. Let the fairies take her and do what they liked. Her future – what was left of it – lay tattered under madness and loss anyway.

A splash interrupted the rhythm of the waves, and then a distant shout. She uprighted herself in the water, and turned to see Simon surfacing a few feet away. He swam towards her, his stroke stronger than it had any right to be.

The water grew colder, bone-chilling. She moved her legs quicker but the water moved in cold ribbons, tugging at her ankles. Each tug took her out of the calmer waters, towards the rocks where currents competed in whirlpools and eddies.

She sank down, head dunked under the water, and had to fight to its surface. Her dress dragged at her. She kicked off the left shoe, and then the right, yelling as the shoe pulled the skin of her heel with it.

"Amy!" Simon fought through the surf towards her, but she could see how one arm was lifted higher as he swam, how he was tiring. Still, he came forwards, his eyes on hers, fighting the currents. Three feet away. Two.

The air grew sharp, and the sea-tang stronger. Shadows broke from the rocks and cut off the warm sun. They stretched over the sea, blanketing the waters so they were brackish. She ducked out of their way, felt one graze her breast, a coldness that reached for her heart.

She was close enough. Time to be taken. She opened her hands. For a moment, the acorn sat cradled in her palm, and then the tide washed over and took it. The acorn slipped into the waters, a golden glint on the surface. It started to sink, its gold turning dappled and dark. A strange peace came over her. She'd decided, for herself, what was best.

A hand of water rose from the sea, a great cascade that made her turn her head away with a yell. Water flooded back to the ocean, drumming all around her, filling her ears, her eyes, her mouth. She struggled to stay afloat but barely knew which way was up.

The cascade ended. The plume of water fell back to the sea, her acorn carried on its tip, like a jewel. This time, when it went into the sea, it didn't sink but ran over the water to the boat, handed from Shee to Shee.

The boat listed. A sucking noise announced the rush of water as its hull lifted. The sea turned back to rusty orange under it.

The worlds stay apart. The voice was one she'd never heard before, full of a deep kindness she wanted to embrace. *The worlds are safe.*

Something dropped into the sea before her, small and iridescent. A shell petal. It floated for a moment before melting. Another fell, fading through blues and greens. And another, showering down around her. The boat shed its shell-skin, returning to a rusting hulk, staining the water orange once more.

Realisation hit. She forced herself towards the ship. She had to go with it. She'd made her decision. There was no place for her in the real world anymore.

Her hand closed on nothing. The high smell of rust, like blood in her mouth, faded. She tried to catch one of the shells. She wanted something to hold onto. Proof, perhaps, of what had happened. But the shells were gone as if they'd never been there. If they *had* ever been there.

She opened her hands in the water, splaying her fingers. Without proof, how could she sound anything other than crazy? Without proof, how would she know she wasn't?

Simon had almost reached her, forcing his way through the last couple of yards. His face was pale, a drain of exhaustion, but he was still swimming, his legs still kicking up a strong splash. If he turned back now, he could make it to shore.

She opened her mouth to tell him to leave, but the water washed over her, and into her mouth. She pushed upwards, lifting herself. A wave sloshed and broke around her, sucking her down. She tried to push through the surf, but her legs were heavy and cold.

Another wave splashed into surf as she gulped a breath. The water filled her mouth and nose, dark and briny. Her legs hit against something hard: the cliff was right behind her. Her left leg scraped along the rock, opening the gash from yesterday. Salt water rushed into the cut, making her yell at the sharp pain.

Another wave slapped down, taking her full on the face. Choking, she tried to grab the rocks, but the water pulled her away and then back to crash hard against them.

Her back exploded with sharp pain. The relentless tide pulled her forward again. She tried to twist to protect herself, but the water's force slammed against the rocks. Water slopped over her face, holding her in its cold grasp, and sucked her down once more.

There was no way back, to either world. She didn't have the strength to keep swimming, and Simon would never reach the beach if he had to carry her through the water as well as himself.

This sea, stinging her lips and flooding her mouth, was the end.

THE UNDERCURRENT TUGGED at Simon's legs, twining around his muscles. Amy's head came up, but another wave smothered her and she disappeared.

He was out of time. He forced his injured shoulder to move faster, gritting his teeth. Amy's dress spread out, a billow of cloud on the surface of the water. He heaved the last two strokes and reached for her, fighting the material of her dress, pushing it to the side. She came to the surface, gasping, but she'd barely managed a breath when she sank again.

He snagged her arm, bracing one foot against the rocks, and pulled, yelling at the God-awful pain tearing through his shoulder.

She kicked her legs. Broke the surface and gulped air. He gathered her against him, into his arms, and forced them both away from the rocks, towards the open sea. He thrashed his feet, putting every bit of strength he had into his kicking. Amy was kicking, too, stronger than he'd imagined her to be. Her eyes met his and they were wide and scared.

"There's no boat!" she shouted.

No shit. He tried to tell her he knew, but he could only choke water. She shivered against him. He could feel the bones in her wrist under her thin skin, how slender they were and something moved in him; they were so close to making it back. He just had to hold on another few minutes, for both of them, and fight the tide a little harder.

They broke free of the cross-currents at the base of the rocks. Hope flared and he powered forwards, ignoring the wrenching pain in his shoulder. The current supported him, making it easier, and he was sure the beach was in reach.

A cross-current caught him and dragged at him. He fought to free himself, but the water pulled him back another couple of feet. *Calm.* He waited, conserving his energy, for the next in-tide and took a long stroke, working with the water. It worked, for a moment, until the ebbing tide carried him back, further than before.

"Can you swim?" he asked. "We need to swim."

She nodded, with just the slightest hesitation. He tightened his grip on her waist – if he let her go, he'd be lucky to get to her again. He paddled his legs, using his good arm to pull them through the water. She kicked, too, thank God; he wouldn't get both of them back to shore on his own.

The tide pulled them one way and then the other, but each cycle took the pair farther out to sea. Simon fought it, teeth gritted, striving for the beach, the way he'd focus on the try-line on a Saturday morning; everything concentrated, distracted by nothing.

"Kick harder," he said. If they went further out to sea, they'd have no hope. He aimed for the beach, but made no headway. His shivers matched Amy's. At least the cold had numbed his shoulder.

Amy turned in his arms, and almost freed herself. "I'm holding you back."

"Stay still." He tightened his grip.

She tried to loosen his fingers. "You have to go. We can't both drown."

A wave slopped over his face, into his mouth, making him cough against it. Another came, quicker than he expected and he sank a little. *Fight. Keep going; use your strength.* The beach was still too far away: they were not going to make it.

If they could hold out long enough the coastguard would get to the cove. Twenty minutes, maybe, or half an hour depending where the boat was – a long time to last without draining their strength.

If anyone saw them from the beach and called for help. He clutched Amy tight to him, sharing what little warmth they had between them, and scanned the horizon for anyone within shouting distance.

There was no one between the cove and the harbour in the village: no people, no boats, nothing but grey rocks, echoing the coldness of the water. In the distance the town's strand, full of families enjoying what would likely be one of the last good days before winter hit, was hopelessly far away. Even if someone saw them, they'd assume their bobbing heads were a rock, their waving arms some sort of bird.

Fear came, colder than the sea. Thoughts circled, ones he didn't want to face, but had no way of hiding from. He was going to die here, chasing a mad woman who'd stabbed him. It could only happen to him.

He wanted to tell Amy he was sorry, that she'd have been better not meeting him at the waterfall but someone more able, someone who'd have taken care of her, but his strength was gone, and it was enough to hold her against him, keep her afloat in the water and make it easier for her. He stretched out his body, surrendering to the ebb of the tide.

Another splash of sea on his face. He was cold, so cold he didn't care. He should have kept his clothes on. Except Amy, dressed, was shivering just as badly. She lay, stretched along the length of him. Tired, like him. A wave lifted him out to sea. It was easier now he'd stopped fighting. The wash of a wave covered his face, and he spat some of the water out, but swallowed more.

It didn't matter. His hold on Amy loosened, and that didn't matter either. Not here, under the clear sky.

Chapter Thirty-Two

T HE TAXI PULLED up at the harbour. Mark wrenched the door open and took off at a run. He darted into the caves, where a small crowd had gathered at the mouth of the cove. A police car had also pulled up – they'd got his message, then. He'd done something right. As he ran past the main cave, he saw a larger car parked; presumably the one Amy had taken.

The crowd were pointing at the sea. *Oh, Christ.* He sped up, his chest burning, and his dad caught up with him, belying his age. They both shouldered to the front of the crowd.

"No further." A policeman put his hand out, stopping him. "The coastguard will need access."

"It's my sister." Mark tried to peer past the man, but could see nothing other than the rock-cove and water beyond.

"And my daughter." Dad pushed past and ran forward. "Amy!"

"Is she there?" asked Mum. "Did I give her enough time

to bring Matty?"

"You…?" He thought of his mother over the years, her tales to Amy about the fairies, her constant reassurance that Amy shouldn't be scared, that nothing could ever happen to her. This time, when his anger came, it broke. "You bitch," he said, his voice loud enough to bring some of the watchers' attention to him. "I hope you rot." He couldn't believe what he felt, what he was saying. "I hope, when we get Amy back, she cuts you off. I have."

"Of course you have." She was maddenly calm. "I primed you to do that. You held her here too well, you and your dad. You had to be off-side."

She had played them all like fools. He cramped over, the knowledge a physical pain. How long had it been going on? How much of his childhood had been real? She'd loved him, he was sure, as a child. *Hadn't she*? Or had it been readying him for the moment she cut him off, knowing it would hurt more if he cared, and damage him further. Knowing if she hurt him enough, pushed him away, he'd leave her with Amy and not come back. He took a step forward, fists bunched, just about holding onto the thought that if she'd been a bloke he'd have floored her, but he couldn't, not his mother.

"Mark!" His dad's voice cut through the anger, raw and urgent. "She's out there. Amy is. And the lad."

He turned, heart leaping. "They're okay?" He ran to the beach and joined his father, standing beside the policeman. Shoulder by shoulder, they made their way over the last of the rocks. Two figures drifted in the water, well out from the beach.

"Shit." He pulled his shirt off and dropped it onto the rocks.

The policeman grabbed his shoulder. "You can't go in after her."

Mark shook his hand off. The hell he couldn't.

Another man stepped forward, bearded and smelling of brine. "I know these waters." The man shaded his eyes, his eyes calculating. "The tide's on the turn. You'd never make it back in."

"Where are the coastguard?" asked his dad.

"They're round the headland," the sailor said. "They've been called."

They didn't have time to wait. Mark went to stride into the water, but this time his father stopped him. "We can't. Not this way."

His father knew these waters, too. He'd sailed this part of the coast for years, before he'd moored up in Strangford permanently and decided to get pissed for a living instead.

"What, then?" asked Mark, his voice cracking. The figures already seemed further out than they had been just a minute ago.

"The harbour." His dad pushed back up the beach, ignoring any questions. Mark followed at a run.

"Where is she?" Mum grabbed him. "Has she come back? Is Matty with her?" She stopped, looking out to sea. Her hand went to her mouth, and the colour drained from her face. "Phil." The word sounded strangled. "Why is she still out there? Why isn't she coming back?" She scraped her way over the rocks. "Why haven't they brought him back?"

Mark grabbed her arm and thrust her forward. "She's where *you* put her." He ran after his dad, out to the harbour.

"Fuck it," said Dad. He looked at the boats in the harbour, moored up and listing. "Whatever Amy can do, we can do better…" He started down the ladder to the nearest, ignoring shouts for him to stop. Mark glanced back at the policeman, gave a helpless shrug, and followed his dad.

IT WAS AKIN to being rocked to sleep. Water splashed, then broke over his face. There was a strange rhythm to it. Lifted by a wave, the soft descent, another splash. Water in his mouth, up his nose, and then he was lifted out again and crested for a moment.

He should care, but didn't. He should do something to get back to shore, but couldn't. The sun was sharp, even through closed eyes. A slop of water drowned his face.

He could hear someone's voice rising and falling, muffled by the water. A banshee, he decided. Had to be: heralding their deaths. He wished he could tell Amy – then she'd know that she'd been right, and the fairies did exist, but his mouth didn't want to move.

The water embraced him. Slowly, he felt himself sink.

"MOVE OVER. I'M going to break it." Dad lifted the crowbar he'd unearthed from the dinghy's underseat storage and wrenched the top of the engine box off. "Get ready to throttle her back when I tell you."

"Quick." Mark stood, hand on the throttle, eyes scanning, trying to place the cove. Even though the autumn sea would be warmer than usual, this was the North Atlantic. Warmth was relative.

There was a crash and a splintering noise. "Nearly there." His dad dug out the emergency starter rope. He threw the fuel valve on the primer around to 180 and squeezed the primer a few times, his eyes narrowed, assessing. He fixed the knot of the starter rope onto the flywheel. "Been years since I've tried this." He gave a sharp nod to Mark. "Ready?"

"Ready." It was never going to work. He glanced back at the caves and saw the policeman holding the crowd back. Good man, he'd figured it out. Mark gave him a nod of thanks. May was right – the police in this area had sense, and if it took breaking an outboard engine to save two lives, so be it.

His dad pulled the rope. The engine roared to life, the sudden throttling nearly knocking Mark off his feet, but he managed to throttle back, only to be shoved aside by his dad taking the helm and turning the boat out of the harbour and into the open sea.

THE COLD HAD vanished, as had the weight of Amy's body. Simon managed to open his eyes, crusty from the salt and the sun. Amy had floated away and turned over in the water and that wasn't right. She should be looking at the sun. He tried to reach out and turn her over, but nothing worked anymore.

Arms grabbed him, strong arms, bringing him out of his stupor. He reached out one hand and snagged Amy's wrist, pulling her to him.

"Don't let her go," said a voice. "Christ, big man, you're too heavy to be dragging around."

Mark. Skinny Mark. Simon thrashed, trying to help.

"Stay still, for fuck's sake!" The voice was loud. Simon

was hauled out of the water, and Mark tried to wrestle him into a dinghy.

"Take Amy first." He found the strength to pass her up, and grabbed the side of the dinghy with his other hand. Mark pulled her into the boat. She didn't help, but slid bonelessly in.

Mark grabbed his hands and pulled Simon in, heaving him over the side. From the helm, a Ben Gunn lookalike gave a quick nod, and throttled the boat up, heading into the mouth of the mockingly-close cove. Amy's dad, he presumed.

Simon managed to get to his knees. He coughed like he'd never stop, retching water up, more than he'd ever imagined possible. It spilled onto the bottom of the boat, foaming against a film of sand. Beside him, Mark had Amy in his arms, and was hitting her on the back. She wasn't coughing.

"Dad," he said. "She's in a bad way."

"Amy!" Amy's mum ran forwards. Amy's dad – Phil, he remembered – threw the rope to one of the waiting men, who caught it and used a rock as an anchor, wrapping the rope around it. They pulled the boat up the shingle beach.

"Emma," said Phil, his voice carrying an edge of warning. She stopped at the edge of the water, mouthing no, no, no.

"Let me see." Phil pushed his son to the side. His daughter lay, unmoving. He leaned his head over her. "Amy, come on, love." He breathed into her mouth.

Simon tried to speak, to tell her to breathe, to try, but he coughed again, and brought up more seawater. Mark, crouched by her, held up a warning hand. "Stay there."

Simon shook his head and crawled over. He took Amy's

hand. It was cold and still. He squeezed it, willing her to feel him. "Come on," he whispered. "Fight. Like you did in the garden. Fight." He held her hand, gulping air that she needed, air he'd do anything to give her. "You can't die." She should live. She should have a life of her own, not the fairies'.

"Come on, Amy." Mark's voice was low, barely breathed. "Don't go, love. We're all here."

A keening sounded from the beach; a sound of such pure loss that Simon wanted to bury his head in the sand and not listen. Emma was on her knees, her head back. She pulled at her hair, tearing it out in clumps. A woman took her hands, trying to stop her, but she pulled free and trailed her nails down her face, leaving long lines. A policewoman pushed her way over to her.

"No," Emma yelled. "She was supposed to come back!"

Simon turned to Amy. Phil was leaning over her, his face grey.

"Come on," he said. His voice was firm. "Amy, breathe."

She gave a cough, just a little one. Simon squeezed her hand. *Fight.* Phil touched her face. "Come on, love. Good girl."

Water bubbled from her mouth. Her dad and Mark turned her onto her side, pulling her hand from Simon, and she was sick, her shoulders heaving as she brought up the seawater. It was brackish and green. When she stopped, she rolled onto her back and stared up at the sky.

"Help her sit up, Mark," said Phil. He had rocked back onto his knees, making the boat sway. His eyes were focused on his daughter.

Mark got his arms under Amy's shoulders and she

managed to stagger to her feet. She looked all around the crowd, then paused at her keening mum. Her eyes cleared and she looked shocked.

"Mum?" She coughed, was sick again, gulped air. "I'm sorry."

Her eyes met Simon's. He knew what he must look like – half-naked, his hair salt-filled, hanging around his face, bloodied all down his chest. He'd scare the life out of her, most likely.

Her eyes widened, and she reached for him. "I'm sorry," she said. "I –"

He touched her face, his palm against the curve of his jaw. Her warm, living skin was warm under his touch.

"Shh," he said. "It wasn't you. I saw."

Chapter Thirty-Three

M ARK STRAIGHTENED UP. Amy cuddled against Simon, refusing to be parted from him. His good arm tightened around her shoulder; the other hung by his side, a long gash vivid and red against his drained skin. They made their way past the crowd in the caves, who were beginning to disperse now the show was over, into the relative warmth of the largest cavern, where the car still sat abandoned.

It was hard to tell who looked more beaten up. Amy's legs were badly cut and the gash on Simon's shoulder was deep and torn. The rate things were going, a triage nurse would be needed before the police.

"Is there an ambulance coming?" he asked the policeman overseeing the rope being wound in.

"On its way." His face grew stern. "Once she's been seen, we'll have to interview her."

They'd deal with that when it came up. Mark turned away. His parents were at the end of the shingle, near the big cave, his dad talking to Mum. He had his hands out, open, as if pleading, presumably trying to calm her. It didn't seem to be working – whilst her awful keening had ended, she was wringing her hands, scratching the back of one with the nails of the other. Her thinking might have been screwed-up, but there'd been no mistaking the loss in her cries, or the distress she was still in. It had cut through his anger, leaving him more confused than ever. Everything she had done had been about love, not vengeance – but how could love have got so twisted?

He couldn't make any sense of it. He walked past his mum and dad, joining Simon and Amy. Simon had gone beyond pale to a sick-green colour. Amy looked like without him to lean against, she'd collapse.

"Come here," Mark said to Amy, and took her from Simon. He led her to the passenger side and helped her onto the seat. He left the door open, to give her some air, and then helped Simon to the back seat. The lad sank into the material, his eyes on Amy. The look had an intensity it felt wrong to intrude on and Mark moved away, leaving them in private. No doubt the police would be here soon; let Amy have a few moments of peace to gather her thoughts.

Jesus, car theft and attempted murder. She'd be charged, at the very least, if not taken into custody. It would be hard to convince anyone she'd been sick enough to take a car and not know what she was doing. His jaw tightened. He was damned if the police would be doing anything to his sister other than confirming her mental history.

He stood at the end of the cave, not quite on guard, so drained that he didn't want to move any further but was content to stand, listening to the waves coming in and out, letting himself be lulled by them.

A noise behind him, the soft scuff of shoes, made Mark

turn. His mother had passed him while he'd been distracted and was standing at the door to the car, where Amy was sitting. Amy got out and faced their mother. Something passed between them, the invisible cord that held Amy and his mother together, the secret part of their relationship no one intruded on.

His mother took a step forwards, still wringing her hands, eyes never leaving Amy, and a tickle of unease started at the back of his neck. He took a step into the cave.

"Amy…" He cleared his throat and raised his voice. His dad was busy on the shingle, having joined the fishermanto help push the boat into the deeper water, his trousers rolled up to the knees. "Be careful."

Amy shook her head, confused. "What do you mean?" And of course she should ask – she didn't know about their changed mother.

"I know you better than anyone." Mum's voice was gentle. She lifted Amy's chin and stared into her eyes.

The intensity of the stare got Mark moving. He angled forwards, not wanting to over-react and make everything bigger than it was, but needing to be nearer. He halted next to Simon's open door, close enough to watch.

Their mother ran her gaze all the way up and down Amy, who seemed resigned to the attention. How many times had her mother had done this over the last few months? Lots, he realised, more than in the past – and she'd always been obsessed with Amy.

His mother's face seemed to relax, the deep lines around her mouth reducing. She rubbed Amy's cheek, leaned in so she was close, and Mark relaxed, sure she was going to hug Amy and tell her everything was all right.

Instead, she sniffed Amy. Her face changed, eyes

narrowing, head shaking. She ran her nail along Amy's cheek, just below her eye. Amy flinched away, but their mother tightened her hold on Amy's chin, digging in against her jawbone. Mark dashed the length of the car.

"Mum!" said Amy, trying to break away but their mother pulled her away from the car and shoved her up against the rock wall. She stood, staring at her, eyes wide, almost disbelieving.

Oh, hell. Mark lunged for them. He remembered Mum's comments from earlier, about Amy's eyes being too dark, her smile too knowing.

"Emma!" yelled Dad, from behind him. "Leave her alone!"

Mum's mouth drew back into a snarl, her eyes flashing with anger.

"No!" she shouted. "It's not Amy."

She held her daughter's shoulders, tight enough for her nails to dig into skin. Her lips were curled back and ugly, her scream one of hatred. Mark dived at her, trying to get between them, but Mum knocked him away with the flat of her elbow, stronger than she should ever be. He stumbled back and fell, hard, onto the rock floor, dazing himself.

She locked her hands around Amy's throat and started to squeeze.

Chapter Thirty-Four

AMY TRIED TO twist away. Her mother's hands were tightening, and she was screaming a wordless something that made no sense. Her mother pulled her round and thrust her towards the barred gate to the garden, now closed to. Momentum carried her backwards, still in her mum's grasp, her feet scrabbling for any hold on the slick rock-surface and she hit the bars, sending a thudding pain through her spine.

"Get off me," Amy gasped, but it was croaked, barely there. She brought her hands up, pulling at her mum's wrists. Black dots danced, distorting everything.

"You're not Amy!" Her mum thrust Amy against the bars again, dazing her.

Amy tried to tell her that she was, of course she was, but the words wouldn't come. Mark staggered to his feet, her dad ran towards her, Simon had got out of the car, but they were all too slow or far away. Her mother's hands tightened further.

Amy tried to fight, kicking, tugging at her mum's arms.

She was slammed against the bars again. Stars whirled in front of her eyes. Dizzy sickness swept through her.

"Emma! That's enough!" Her dad, mercifully, grabbed her mother's shoulders and pulled her back. Amy slumped to the ground, trying to catch her breath.

Her dad yelled. Her mother ducked out of his grasp. Blood dripped down his hand and, dimly, Amy realised she must have bit him. Mum dove for her.

Amy tried to roll away, but her mother was astride her, holding her down. She grabbed Amy's hair and wrenched her head up. Someone yelled and Amy realised it was herself.

Her mother bunched her hands. "Abomination!" she yelled. "Give me back my daughter." She slammed Amy's head against the rock floor. Amy bucked and twisted. The stars turned in a fast circle.

"Mum!"

"Monster!" Her mum was practically frothing at the mouth. Her hands went for Amy's throat again. Amy choked and bucked, but her mum wouldn't be dislodged.

"Get off her, you bitch!" Her dad grabbed Mum from behind, lifting her to her feet. She took Amy with her, dragging her upright.

"Mum," she croaked, but the hold got tighter. Her dad was shouting for Mark to help, Simon, anyone.

Mark pulled their mother away, his fingers prising hers from Amy's neck. She fought, spitting and screaming.

Amy scrambled back. She put her hand to her throat. Mark dragged their mother back, and Dad, a bruise darkening on his temple, helped.

Amy was left alone with Simon. His eyes were wide with shock. He'd been right, in the garden, when he'd said it wasn't her.

The last months fell into place – her mother hadn't been going over the old ground to make Amy face up to her thoughts, or the fairies, or whichever they'd been. She'd been doing it to reinforce her own belief; the more real it was to Amy the less doubt there was in her own mind. She felt cold as she thought back over the years, all the events of her childhood, talked about and talked about until they'd become some sort of fable. It had been going on as long as she remembered, encouraged by her mother. She'd made her go to the wedding in the glen, Amy remembered. She'd bought the house in the woods. She'd *wanted* this to happen.

She limped to the car and slumped against it, too tired to take another step. Simon reached out and put a hand on her arm, but she shook him off. She'd hurt him, and all because of something put into her head. The enormity of that, that she could have killed him – it had taken everything in her not to – was too much for her to deal with.

Her mother fought Mark and Dad, kicking and screaming. She managed to free one arm and pointed at Amy. "Abomination! You're a fake!"

Like hell she was. Amy faced her mum, taking in the twisted hatred of her features, the bared teeth. She looked nothing like the mother Amy recognised.

Doesn't she? The sly voice whispered from the back of Amy's mind, remembering the little looks her mum had given her over the years when she thought Amy wasn't watching. The ones with narrowed eyes, the ones that said something wasn't right. They'd always been fleeting, too fleeting to take the place of the mother who doted on her, who wanted to know everything about Amy: what she thought, what she saw, what she believed. But they'd always been there.

Amy clenched her fists. She felt sick to her stomach. She held up her arm. "Feel me; skin and bones, just like yours."

"You're not like me. You've never been like me since they took you and made you into what you are now. You're one of *them*." She launched herself again, pulling Dad off his feet.

Amy backed away. Jesus, her mother *was* mad.

"Changeling," her mum said.

Amy shook her head. "I'm not!"

"You were taken!" said her mum. "In the glen. Stolen."

When she was a child in the glen. She'd wandered off, down the brook with its slippery pebbles. She'd knocked her head as she fell and had lain in the shallow water, half-aware she was being looked for. Everything else, the fairies, the Queen – that was hazier.

Except the acorn. She remembered picking it up, how it had shone. She'd thought it was pretty, but it had cracked and split in her hand. She thought of the stones at Ossian's grave, how they'd wanted her to use the acorn to break through.

Finally, she thought of the shee – they'd taken the acorn, and then the boat had left. Imagine, her acorn being so strong. Had the Queen reached only to take that talisman? Had Amy angered them simply by not allowing them to take back what was theirs?

She wasn't special. The realisation brought nothing but relief. She was someone who'd wandered into a half-world and had taken something of the fae. She thought of their faces, all like hers, the dark honeyed air of the garden when she hadn't had the acorn.

She'd escaped the fairies as a child, running and running

until she'd found herself back at the brook. Her dad and Mark had left, and it was dark. The only sound had been the water. Its noise had turned to a song, and then voices had called for her, and bright lights had swept from the sky, so bright the fairies would never come near them.

They'd brought her mummy to her, and she'd never told her, or anyone, what really happened. She'd forgotten, until now, the fear of the glen, the sharp knowledge of the fae, the running from them.

Mark approached, their mother behind him, and his face mirrored her own sadness. The night their mother had kicked him out, he'd seemed beaten. She'd begged their mother, after he'd gone, to see what she was doing to him, how much the cold rejection must have hurt. But she'd been sure Mark should be standing on his own two feet. The certainty, always the certainty.

"You changed," said her mum, and the certainty was there again.

"I was four!"

"You *changed*." Her mother made a grab for her, but Mark held her back. Simon put his arm around Amy's waist and pulled her against him. She felt the warmth of his body, his slow breathing, the reality of him, and no one mattered more.

"You're dirty," her mum said. "They've been coming for years, waiting for you to go back. Why haven't you?" Emma fell back against Mark. Her shoulders were shaking. "I wanted my daughter back. She was perfect."

"You're wrong," Simon said. "About everything."

Amy's mouth fell open. She'd tried to kill him. He should hate her. Her mum stared at him, as if hearing it from someone outside the family – and God knew, her dad and Mark had been trying to tell her for years that there was nothing wrong with Amy, nothing that couldn't be made better if she took her damn tablets and let the doctors do their work – made it real.

Simon put his arm around Amy, his muscles tight and taut. He made her feel safe – and she needed that after her mother's attack. He took her face, cupping it in his hands, gentler than she'd imagined anyone to be, and he kissed her, his lips soft, melting into hers, something she'd been waiting for all her life for.

He broke away, smiled, and whispered, "She's perfect."

EPILOGUE

T HE COTTAGE GARDEN was peaceful, making it Amy's favourite place to have coffee all this week. Ever, in fact. She stretched her toes out, letting the sun's rays fall on them. Simon's arm was around her shoulders, his hand draped so that it touched her collarbone. He'd done more than touch her earlier. Warmth spread through her at the thought of his lips leaving no place unexplored. She took a quick look around, made sure they were on their own, and reached up to turn his head to her, until his lips were against hers and soft, opening to welcome her.

A rattle of cups made her break away and flush. Simon didn't redden, he just gave a half-smile that said damn, and flicked his eyes up and down her in the way that promised *later*, and made her a little shivery.

The waitress left their tray on the little table in front of them. The wood on it was flaked, and a wasp lazily landed and buzzed on the other side of it, seeking nesting materials. Simon idly swatted it and it droned off, down the length of a narrow path, past willow fronds and ferns, to land on a weathered bench instead.

Amy lifted the earthen teapot and poured mint tea into a bowled cup. She cradled it in her hands for a moment before sipping. Bliss. On the plate in front of her, a scone and a pot of cream cried out to be eaten.

The smell of Simon's coffee – she'd never known anyone who could drink so much coffee – carried to her, mingling with her mint. He was munching his way through a stack of pancakes with maple syrup and bacon. She'd never known anyone who could eat like him, either. She let her gaze fall, surreptitiously, along the length of his muscled arm. He was putting it to good use. He noticed her glance and raised his eyebrow in a way that made her stomach turn over. She nestled against him and they sat like that for a moment. A peacock, just on the other side of the garden gates, gave a shriek and opened his feathers to full display.

"Show off," said Simon.

"Typical male."

He grinned, but she ignored him. They had three more days up here, buried from anyone who knew them, getting familiar with each other. He could wait.

"How's your mum doing?" he asked. "Did Mark say?"

"Mmmm." She drew in a breath, letting the smells from the herb bed – warm oregano, spicy basil, fresh mint – settle her. She focused for a moment, calming herself. At last she was able to answer. "She's doing okay. She still won't see me, though."

"Maybe it's not a bad thing. Just for a while."

She nodded. The doctors agreed with him. A sense of wrenching loss lanced her, but it passed quicker than it once had. Being without her mother was unfamiliar. She missed having her to talk to, the smell of her perfume, the moments they'd shared shopping for clothes, doing girly things together. Without her, it felt like some part of her was missing.

"I just hope," she said, "that we can past it someday. That we can have some kind of relationship." Except that her mother still thought she was a changeling, placed in vengeance by the fairies when their baby, Matty, had died. It was a messed up cycle of long-held psychosis, something it might take years to cure.

"Remember what your counsellor said. There'll be time to face things, when you're stronger."

She took a sip of tea. She *was* stronger. But not strong enough for that. Not yet.

"What about the chaos twins?" asked Simon, breaking the mood. "Are they still talking?"

Poor Mark: he'd finally fallen apart, blaming himself, so much so that Amy had grown scared that he'd do worse than pick fights. Redemption had come from the unlikeliest of sources. Their dad, having already fought the police charges against her, using doctors' statements to devastating effect, took Mark under his wing. He'd moved into his apartment, distracting his son with his itinerant approach to life. Buying the occasional new t-shirt, Mark had taken to announcing, was not optional. Nor, for that matter, was basic household hygeine.

"Just about." She couldn't live in the sort of chaos they did. She buttered the scone, watching the garden. "Dad's still sober, amazingly."

Silence fell between them. She'd never imagined being able to return to this sort of place, full of hidden corners and dancing flowers.

Simon, ever pragmatic, had gone back to his pancakes.

He didn't see her look down the cobbled path opposite, to where it opened out into a hidden courtyard. She waited, until – there: something fluttered, the same something that had been there each time they'd visited. Her heart missed a beat, watching. A teenage fairy, she was sure. Probably delinquent.

She watched until the fairy flitted away and took a sip of tea to calm herself. She put her hand in Simon's and squeezed. *Don't listen*, he'd said, and that was what she had to hold onto. She'd given the fairies strength with her belief, and she'd never do that again.

The doctors could say what they liked, and claim she'd been mistaken, but she knew the truth. The fairy world was real. Even if it could no longer be reached, she still knew the magical places to look.

It didn't matter, anymore. She was safe. Just as long as she didn't listen.

Acknowledgements

As ever, this will be the equivalent of an Oscar speech. (Grips statuette tightly).

My family and friends who have come to launches, promoted me everywhere, put up with obsessive mutterings about the stories and who are the backbone of every book I've brought out. Special mention to Chris, Becky and Holly who have to live with me hunched over a computer. You rock.

The writing community who support me – on facebook, twitter, on forums (especially the SFFchronicles), at conventions. Without support this wouldn't be possible.

As ever, people have been good enough to read through my early workings of Waters and the Wild and feed back to me about what worked/what didn't and, most importantly, what should never see the light of day. The Hex-men, my writing group, looked at this early on and, as ever, were invaluable in their feedback. But, also, the full-story beta readers: Em Tett, Juliana Spink Mills, Sue Jackson, John Brady and Kerry Buchanan. A special mention to Bryan Wigmore who told me I needed a road trip, who nagged me about a rooooaddd trippppp and who will now see it is, indeed, a road trip.

Thanks too, to the professionals at Inspired Quill, who've worked so hard on this with me. Rebecca Hall for editing, Sara-Jayne Slack for further editorial guidance and more, and to Venetia Jackson for an awesome, awesome cover that I've preened over.

About the Author

Jo writes mostly-dark sci fi and fantasy, sometimes in her native Northern Ireland, sometimes in her space opera world. She's been writing for five years and is the author of The Inheritance Trilogy and Inish Carraig, both sci fi books.

She's joining Inspired Quill with her first fantasy book, a dark fairy tale set in the beguiling Glens of Antrim.

When she's not writing, Jo runs her own management consultancy, juggling work, writing, children, pets and her husband. She also grows her own veg, makes jam and wrangles dragons in her spare time (one of these might not be strictly true).

Find the author via her website: www.jozebedee.com

Or tweet at her: @joz1812

MORE FROM THIS AUTHOR

Inish Carraig

The invasion is over. Humanity has lost.

In Belfast, John Dray protects his younger siblings by working for the local hard man. Set up, he gets sent to the formidable alien prison, Inish Carraig, a fate Henry Carter, the policeman assigned to John, can't stop.

Once there, John discovers a plot which threatens Earth and everyone he loves. To reveal it, he has to get out of the prison – and there is only one person who can help. The stakes are raised for both men – and humanity needs them to act.

A bestseller in Alien Invasion, Inish Carraig is 'blessed with an entirely novel storyline'

– Alexander Stevenson-Kaatsch

Paperback ISBN: 9781516887620

Abendaus Heir

Kare doesn't want to inherit his mother's galactic Empire. He, more than anyone, knows the cruelty she is capable of. But there is no one else who can stand against her.

From hunted child, to the agony of being his mother's captive, his life has never been his own.

His destiny lies in the Empress's city of Abendau. There, he faced her torture chambers, his mind picked apart. He'll have to return if he is ever to forge his own future.

Paperback ISBN: 9780992907754

Available as Paperbacks and eBooks
from all major online and offline outlets.

Lightning Source UK Ltd.
Milton Keynes UK
UKOW04f1250151117
312752UK00001B/161/P